"How is Nora working out?"

It was with the most enthusiasm he had seen from his friend in a long time when Ben answered, "Great. I couldn't have found someone more perfect if I searched the globe. It's like having an invisible mind reader in the house. If I want a drink, it appears. If I am hungry, a plate of food is just there. I drop something on the floor, it's put back. Her culinary skills would rival any high-end restaurant."

"I'm happy you finally found someone to stay," he said, "but what's her story?".

"What do you mean?"

"I only met her for a few minutes, but even I can tell she was running or hiding from something."

Ben's brow furrowed. "What makes you say that?"

"If what you have said about her is true, why is she working for you?"

"Thanks a lot."

"I don't mean you're not a nice guy, but why wouldn't she go to some place where her talents can be appreciated? What do you really know about her?"

Ben leaned in toward Brian. "I know she is darn good at what she does. She has been honest and reliable. What more do I need to know? Stop looking for problems where none exist."

Tattered Hearts

by

C. Ellen Culverwell

This is a work of fiction. Names, characters, places, and incidents are either the product of the author's imagination or are used fictitiously, and any resemblance to actual persons living or dead, business establishments, events, or locales, is entirely coincidental.

Tattered Hearts

Cover Art by *The Wild Rose Press, Inc.*

The Wild Rose Press, Inc.
PO Box 708
Adams Basin, NY 14410-0708
Visit us at www.thewildrosepress.com

Publishing History
First Edition, 2024
Trade Paperback ISBN 978-1-5092-5293-0
Digital ISBN 978-1-5092-5294-7

Published in the United States of America

Dedication

For Claudia

Chapter One

Nora Manning packed two large suitcases in the trunk of her car. She condensed her entire life in its contents. When she slammed the trunk shut, she paused with her head bowed as if in prayer. Rain began to beat down on her head, saturating her hair and dripping down her face. She made no attempt to cover herself. Her chest heaved as she drew in a deep breath before taking one final look at the old inn which meant so much to her. She carried in her heart the precious memories made within its walls. There were the painful ones she vowed to leave behind.

Her dear friend Marjorie stood on the sweeping wrap-around porch and waved a sorrowful goodbye. She shouted to be heard above the claps of thunder, "You always have a home here."

Nora opened her car door but before sliding behind the steering wheel placed her fingers to her lips and blew Marjorie a kiss. The women shared a relationship of unconditional trust and loyalty. Nora depended on her friend for discretion and the support needed to leave. After she started the car, she sat frozen with her eyes fixated on the road before her. Foot by yard by mile she watched the only town in which she ever lived disappear in her rearview mirror. When she reached the road sign which read, *You are now leaving Darling, Pennsylvania,* she pulled her car to the side of the road and sobbed for an hour. When she was through, she made a promise to herself to never cry again for the life she left behind. The necessity to free herself from her painful past propelled her forward. Life unknown clawed at her insides, yet knowing there was nothing left for her in her hometown made leaving the right decision. Where she went did not matter so long as it was someplace else.

With no plans, a full tank of gas, and a few meager possessions, she traveled light. She wanted nothing to slow her down or remind her of what she left behind. She pointed the vehicle north and kept driving. She barely noted her surroundings. The rain subsided and the sun began to shine highlighting the colorful wildflowers dotting the roadside. She paid them little heed; sightseeing was low on her list of priorities. She passed through one town after another and stopped only to top off her gas tank or buy a bottle of water. She was numb to everything, which included hunger. She pressed on.

Sometimes she wondered if she lost her mind to leave with no plans, no future, and no one to love her. Oddly, she found something seductive and freeing in her lack of an agenda. The first town she found before darkness fell was as good as any other. Tired both in body and soul, she needed to rest and gather her thoughts. She spotted a large brightly lit sign for an efficiency motel. The grounds were neatly mowed, and gardens planted with shrubs and flowers. It lacked elegance, but the attention taken to its neat appearance allowed her to assume management took pride in it. Confident the interior rooms shared the same attention to detail, she stopped for the night. She parked in front of the office to inquire about a room. At the front desk Nora was greeted by an elderly desk clerk, occupied with a crossword puzzle. She was wearing a nametag which identified her as Ruth. She looked up with a smile and an engaging glint in her eyes. "Good evening."

In her characteristic subdued voice Nora replied, "Good evening. Do you have any vacancies?"

"Several. Each is similar, a bedroom and living-dining-kitchenette. How long do you plan to stay?"

"My plans are open ended. Do you have a time limit?"

Ruth reached for the guest register, sliding it toward Nora. "No, most of our guests are people who need temporary lodging for business purposes. There are numerous large companies in the City of Cheswick."

"Cheswick?" Nora repeated. Her escape to nowhere left her ignorant of her location. She never so much as consulted a map during her entire road trip. She knew she was somewhere in Central New York State, but nothing beyond her general location.

"Not familiar?" Ruth asked not waiting for a response. "The larger companies contract with us to accommodate extended stay employees. Eventually they move to the area unless it's for short-term employment."

Nora nodded. "So, they aren't transients?"

She snorted a laugh. "No, dear. This isn't a 'no tell motel.' "

Nora worried she might have insulted the older woman. She did not mean to give the impression she questioned the integrity of the motel as she always went out of her way to say and do all the right things. "I'm sorry. I didn't mean to suggest anything derogatory."

Again, Ruth laughed. "I didn't take it that way. If you are passing through and know nothing about us, it's a reasonable concern. I'm just as guilty of sizing up people who come through the door. We don't put up with any nonsense around here."

Nora was relieved by Ruth's candor. She seemed direct and kind, exactly what she needed. Her lips slightly curved up in a half smile. "Do I measure up?"

"You do indeed. Do you wish to keep a credit card on file? The rates are different depending on the length of your stay."

Nora scrawled her name in the register leaving her address blank. "That will be fine. If my stay is extended, I will let you know."

It was impossible for Nora to supply Ruth with her length of stay when she didn't even know herself. She was at the disposal of no one. Ruth handed her a key with a suite number. Nora pulled her car around in front of the door and unloaded the suitcases. She was correct in her assumption that the rooms would reflect the exterior. They were spotless, and although the furniture was well worn, it was polished to a fine sheen. She collapsed on the bed in complete exhaustion and slept straight through until ten o'clock the next morning. She never remembered a time in which she allowed herself such a luxury. Mentally she needed every minute of sleep. When she awoke, she was momentarily dazed by the unfamiliar surroundings. When her head cleared, she braced herself for a new day. She showered, changed her clothes, and headed for the motel office; Ruth was still at the desk.

"You must sleep here," Nora said with an amused tenor.

"That's the curse of being the owner. My husband and I live next door. We take turns at the desk and our grandchildren help us to make a little extra money."

"A family affair, how nice for you."

"It's a blessing, *sometimes,* but we like it."

Nora came to her reason for stopping at the office. "Is there a place nearby to eat?"

"Certainly. You haven't been in the town yet?"

Nora shook her head.

"Okay, this is the main drag," she said and pointed her finger to the door. "You can't get lost, just head on up the road and see for yourself. There are places fancier than others and a couple of chain restaurants. I personally prefer the locals, but at least with a chain restaurant you always know what to expect. The village of Bartholomew has something for everyone."

Nora took her advice and headed toward the village. She had no idea what to expect. She was pleasantly surprised. As the main road led her closer to Bartholomew, she was surrounded by picturesque tree lined streets. There were meticulously kept homes from a prior century and parks filled with playground equipment, benches, and duck ponds. She liked the feel as well as the aesthetics of the area. There was a peaceful aura to it. She took her time and drove up and down the side streets. Like all towns, the neighborhoods enjoyed varying economic degrees but none she considered undesirable.

Eventually, she spotted a small restaurant with a patio overlooking an elementary school. It was there she chose to dine. On her way in she grabbed a newspaper from the vendor box and was promptly greeted by a young and clearly pregnant waitress. She smiled and asked, "Inside or patio?"

Nora looked past her outdoors. "I think the patio might be nice."

She was ushered outside to a table covered by a canopy. She discovered she was the only patron seated on the pleasant patio. It suited her. Nora was by nature a shy person, but especially so in an unfamiliar town where she was acquainted with no one. She opened the laminated menu and scanned her choices.

"You've got your choice of breakfast or lunch," the waitress said.

Nora chose lunch. If she consumed a larger meal, she need not worry about eating again until later, allowing her time to explore her options. She was receptive to anything which may interest or distract her from her life. As she dined, she briefly checked the local headlines and then flipped to the employment section. Her need for a job had less to do with income than it did with keeping her body and mind occupied. When the waitress brought her food, she noticed Nora was searching the employment section.

"If you are looking for a job, there is an employment agency in Cheswick. They have an excellent reputation. I have friends who have gotten jobs through the Holder Employment Agency." She pointed to the agency's number on the help wanted ad and told her to try them.

Nora circled their phone number and after finishing her lunch called them. The agency told her their primary clients were looking for temporary help. It was common for the hours to increase to full time if the employee was productive. The person she spoke with suggested she stop in and fill out an application. They gave her an address which Nora programmed into the GPS on her phone.

It was not a long drive, fifteen minutes at most. The city of Cheswick was small as cities go but she saw a vast number of office buildings. She learned later it was a large banking and investment hub for the region. It was in one such building she found the employment agency. She explained she had called earlier, and the receptionist handed her an application to fill out listing all her job experiences and references.

The receptionist escorted her to a small cubicle where she filled in the pertinent information. She answered no questions of a personal nature; the less she explained about herself the better. Standard applications often ask for information not required under employment laws, thus, she avoided them. She left the home address section blank, giving only her cell phone number. When she was through, she handed it back to the receptionist. "The manager generally reviews applications every afternoon. You may receive a call later today or tomorrow."

"That will be fine. I'm available any time."

She returned to the motel to read the newspaper from cover to cover to glean information about the region. It was more cosmopolitan than her hometown, but in many ways, similar. Cheswick looked to be on the forefront of everything trendy, however the suburban town of Bartholomew had a quiet dignity to it. It did not take her long to figure out the affluent residents enjoyed the small-town life, while still being within a short distance of the city amenities. It was a typical scenario in many locales—the smaller homes with no backyards, narrow streets, and crime sent the affluent to the suburbs. The next day Nora continued her exploration while waiting for a response from the employment agency. She traveled through rural farming communities. It had a familiar feel. Her former home was in a simple country village surrounded by orchards and fields. It had a comforting effect, but ultimately it was a matter of complete indifference to her where she lived. She still had no plans and for the first time in her life she was willing to let fate take its course.

In the late afternoon she received a phone call from the owner of the agency, asking her to come in for an interview at her earliest convenience. Since there was nothing to inconvenience her, she said she was available at once. She hoped it pleased the agency manager, it meant they had a person who was serious about working. Too often applicants did not want a job. They were satisfying an unemployment agency, welfare departments, or parents tired of their kids sitting around the house. It was a common complaint among employers, and an experience familiar to Nora while working at the inn.

After being shown into the manager's private office, Nora scanned the room. Everything in it was minimalistic and organized. The woman standing at the opposite side of the desk gave every impression of being the same about all aspects of her life. She was friendly but not personable as she extended her hand. "I am Katherine Holder. I read your application carefully and have already called your reference." She made a gesture toward a chair inviting Nora to be seated. Nora sat erect and attentive on the edge of the chair. She fidgeted when Ms. Holder told her she had vetted her prior to the scheduled interview. Ms. Holder continued, "I understand you operated an inn." She looked down at her notes. "In Darling Pennsylvania. Where is that?"

"It's a small town in northern Pennsylvania on the New York border," she said offering no added details.

"What exactly were your duties?"

"Pretty much everything. I cooked, cleaned, and on occasion did the gardening. My preference was as the inn's chef."

Ms. Holder's voice rose half an octave. "You attended culinary school?"

She did not exaggerate her accomplishments and remained modest in her reply. "It would be misleading to suggest I am a trained chef, but I have a passion for cooking, and I have taken several courses at a culinary school near where I worked."

"If your former employer"— She looked down at her notes again. —"Marjorie Pinkowski, is correct, your culinary skills were very well known in the area."

God Bless Marjorie. "It is something I genuinely enjoyed and gave it my full attention. I suppose you might call it artistic expression."

For the first time Ms. Holder smiled. "I make it a point of checking out my potential employees and clients. I feel an obligation to both, to make certain each are who and what they claim."

Unnerved by the statement, Nora said nothing. She did, however, respect Ms. Holder's diligence. Too often employment agencies' concerns are only for the employer. It was nice to know they also considered the applicant's safety.

"I Googled the inn, the owner, and the phone

numbers to see if they matched the one you gave me; they did. I have also done a background check on you and found no criminal record."

Nora nodded but remained reserved. Knowing everything checked out, her posture became less rigid. She expected any responsible employer to do the same thing.

"In addition, I also asked Mrs. Pinkowski why you left a position where you were apparently so highly regarded."

Nora was careful to show no reaction.

"Mrs. Pinkowski told me it was not for any reason involving your employment. I am obliged to ask you the same question." Her gaze was intense, giving Nora the impression she was looking for any hint of discomfort.

"It was time for me to move on. I am looking for something different and new."

Her answer was sufficient. Temporary agencies were not known for digging into applicants' pasts. If they were satisfied with what they found, no further inquiry was necessary. There were a variety of reasons people needed temporary employment, a divorce, or the end of a heartbreaking or abusive relationship. It did not matter if Nora checked out to be who she purported herself to be. She had used the services of temp agencies when shorthanded at the inn. Nora was counting on no further inquiry.

Katherine Holder sat back in her chair and folded her hand over her midsection. "I'll be honest with you, Ms. Manning, at this time I don't have an open position commensurate with your skills. I do have an opening for a housekeeper-cook in a private residence."

Squirming in her chair, Nora fidgeted with her purse strap. She did not want to be in a family environment. She cringed thinking about satisfying small children or a particular wife and husband with endless demands. At the inn, she met a passing group of happy travelers who did not make unreasonable demands. If they did, they were free to go elsewhere. She related this concern but in a diplomatic fashion. "I am very fond of children, but I don't believe I am best suited to the intimacy of caring for a family."

"I can respect that, but this is a slightly different circumstance. This position is with a single gentleman. He requires light housekeeping and a cook. As an added benefit the position includes a private suite."

Nora's voice quivered. "It's a live-in position?"

"Yes, but I can personally vouch for him. He is a financial analyst and often employs our agency for temporary help. The pay is generous. He makes no unreasonable demands, however having said that, we have never been able to keep a person there for more than a few weeks."

"Why?" Nora asked more out of curiosity than concern. "Does he have a difficult personality?"

"No," she said with assurance. "It is quite the opposite. He is a very private person and does not wish to interact with the domestic help, or for that matter, few others. The feedback I have gotten from the women I have sent to work in his home has been consistent. They say he is very respectful, but it is much like working in a mausoleum. Frankly, they were bored, and any attempt to engage him in conversation was politely rebuked. He makes Calvin Coolidge seem like a chatterbox." She laughed at her own joke.

Nora did not laugh. "I can appreciate that."

The woman looked deep into her eyes and said, "I believe you do. I will fax over your resume to him and then call you if he wishes to interview you. I can almost guarantee he will. Even though we have been less than successful in finding him the right person, we have an excellent working relationship with his business endeavors. If he hires you, it will be a full-time position and you will be working directly for him. We take a finder's fee from the employer under these circumstances. I do intend on keeping your resume on file in the event something more suitable to your experience becomes available."

It sounded perfect to her, quiet and impersonal. "That is very kind of you, but I'm certain this will work."

Ms. Holder cocked her head to one side and snorted. "From you lips to God's ear. I do not see an address on your application. Where are you staying in the event I have some other paperwork?"

"I'm temporarily staying at the Maple Leaf Lodge."

"On Route 5?"

"Yes."

"Good, that's not more than ten minutes from my client's residence. I will give you details if he wants the interview. Well then—" She stood up to shake Nora's hand. "—I hope this will be mutually beneficial. We will be in touch one way or another."

Nora shook her hand and thanked her, leaving with the first sense of contentment she had known in almost a year. She decided to take advantage of the kitchenette in her room and bought easy to prepare food at the market. She had limited capacity to cook, but the challenge alone was a welcome diversion. As she ate, she clicked on the television to watch the local news. She was more interested in the commercials than area events. They gave her an insight into the region's points of interest and local products and services. She had lived in only one region her entire life and realized the necessity to familiarize herself with something new. She was hundreds of miles from home and things were bound to be different.

The next morning, she received a phone call from the employment agency telling her she was expected to be at an interview at four p.m. that same afternoon. They gave her a name and address but no other instructions.

Nora was a detail oriented person in all aspects of her life. She did not want to leave anything to chance and decided to check out the address. She did not wish to appear rude or indifferent by being late because she got lost. Setting her GPS, she easily found the house. It was situated on a cul-de-sac in a clearly affluent area. The house with its neighboring homes was gigantic, but just short of being a mansion. Each home was distinct in architecture but screamed wealth from their fountains to luxury cars in their driveways. The only activity she saw was lawn service trucks and trailers busily manicuring the yards of all the neighboring houses. It was the first time she hoped her interview would be successful. She longed for the peace and solitude of losing herself in a new job.

After assuring herself she knew where she was going, she ventured out to the immediate business district. She found grocers, drug stores, dry cleaners, and every other amenity which she might need. She was nothing if not prepared for her interview.

Chapter Two

Nora returned to her motel room and rummaged through her suitcase. She had limited clothing options. She chose dress slacks and a blouse. She became self-conscious of the weight she lost in the past year. Her clothes hung from her thin frame. At thirty-five she worried it made her look worn and older than her years. She was not a great beauty but possessed the pretty girl-next-door quality. She ran her fingers through her mousy colored hair and grimaced. She tried to decide whether to wear it up or down? It was at a nuisance length, barely long enough to pull back but that was what she did. She held her breath as she took a final look in the mirror to see if she was presentable. She decided it did not matter how she looked if she was well groomed and polite. She was not able to remember the last time she took a second glance at herself. She became a living ghost in her own life, passively existing but not actually living.

Before she left her room, she double checked his name, Benjamin Stafford. If she had a computer, she may have been tempted to research him, however, she thought a fresh first impression was best. She wanted to be judged on her merits, so she decided to extend the same courtesy to him. She had confidence in the employment agency, apparently, he did as well, judging by the prompt interview request.

She was thankful she checked the address prior to her interview. She wanted to be punctual, it was one of her most dependable qualities. She considered tardiness a lack of respect. She did not tolerate it in others and would not be guilty of it herself. As she drove up the cobblestone driveway and stopped in front of the house, she found herself anxious. She was surprised she felt that way, because it was not of paramount importance if she were hired. At this point in her life, she just needed something different and if this did not work out, she'd hop in her car and keep driving.

She traversed the long, brick lined sidewalk and paused at the magnificent leaded glass door. She took a moment to compose herself. She ran her hands down her clothes to smooth them and pulled her shoulders back before she rang the doorbell. A distinguished-looking gentleman answered. He was impeccably dressed in a dark tailored suit which complemented his fit physique. His dark hair was graying at the temples which gave him an air of sophistication. She took him for a man in his mid-forties.

"Mr. Stafford? I'm Nora Manning."

He stepped back pulling the door open. Instead of making a sweeping gesture to invite her in he flicked his hand twice. "Yes, please come in."

She discerned impatient indifference from him. Her years working at the inn prepared her to read people and act in accordance with their personality. She tried not to concentrate on the house or its décor; her focus was solely on following him through the house into his library. He motioned for her to sit in a small leather chair opposite his desk.

"I'd offer you some coffee or tea but frankly that's

why I need a cook and housekeeper; I'm pretty useless in that department." His tone was light but without amusement.

"We can't be good at everything, but fortunately it is one area in which I excel," she said with confidence.

"When can you start?"

Nora's head jerked back. "I beg your pardon?"

He seemed surprised by her surprise. He repeated slowly with distinction, "When can you start?"

She squeaked out a nervous laugh. "Don't you want to ask me any questions?"

His hands, which were resting on his desk, gestured upward. "No, I have complete faith in the employment agency. I have used them dozens of times and I know them to be thorough in their background checks and intuition. It really has not been their fault the earlier housekeepers didn't work out. I just haven't found a person whose temperament is compatible with mine. Do you have any questions for me?"

She had his full attention as he leaned over his desk toward her to wait for any inquiry. "A few, what are your priorities?"

He tilted back in his desk chair, rubbing his chin while he considered her question. "None of the others have asked me that. I would have to say cooking. I do not like to dine out unless it's for business obligations. There is little I don't like but I'd prefer you keep the heavy sauces and bulky carbohydrates to an occasional splurge. Not that I don't love them, but they don't always love me." He smiled for the first time minimizing his detached demeanor.

"What about the house? Are there any rooms or areas off limits?"

He shrugged. "Not really. The only place I am very particular about is this room. I spend the majority of my time here and I have everything arranged exactly the way I need it to function productively. I work, read, and occasionally watch television here. Just keep it clean and tidy. Anything of a professional or personal nature I have locked away. I am not worried about someone working in the house, but I am trusted with the private financial information of clients. I take that responsibility very seriously. As for the rest of the house, you can clean and organize any way which is most efficient for you. Your housekeeping duties will be light. I have a professional cleaning service come in two or three times a year. They do the heavy-duty cleaning` like windows, curtains, washing woodwork, etc. I primarily need your cooking expertise and the agency assured me it is where you excel."

"I do my best. Do you entertain often?" She assumed he must if he wanted a cook.

"Occasionally, but it is usually to reciprocate for an invitation to a friend or client's home. I will give you plenty of notice."

"I would only need a few hours. Cooking at the inn prepared me for a fast turnaround."

"I am seldom home for lunch and when I am, I forage for myself. I like to have breakfast and dinner prepared. I leave for the office at eight and return home at five, but I like to relax in my library and prefer dinner at seven. What days would you like off? I am flexible about that."

She had not thought that far in advance. "Honestly, I don't know. Is it all right if I work here for a while before I decide?"

His tone was flat. "I don't see why not. I am sure we can work something out to our mutual satisfaction. I must leave town tomorrow morning for two days on business."

Nora nodded. "So, you would like me to wait for your return to start?"

He pursed his lips and furrowed his brow. "No." He reached into his desk and pulled out a key, an envelope, and a printed piece of paper. "Here is the key to the house; I have written down the security code, my cell phone number, and an emergency contact, my friend Brian McNair. If there are any problems, he will take care of them for you if you cannot reach me. Here," he said sliding the envelope toward her. "There is five hundred in cash inside. You may need to make purchases for the house to get yourself settled. I have accounts at the supermarket, cleaners, and pharmacy; their names are listed on the paper. Just charge it to me and leave the receipts on my desk along with any mail or packages which may arrive."

She was flabbergasted he was both so trusting and organized.

"I'll show you to your rooms," he said as he stood sliding his chair backward.

Rooms, she thought to herself. She dutifully picked up the items he gave her and followed him through the house, this time noting its splendor. They passed through the kitchen to the back of the house. He opened a door leading to a comfortable sitting room with a private bedroom and connecting bath. It was not large but pleasant and light.

"This is it," he said. "Change whatever you like to make it your own."

She gazed around the room not concerned about its appearance, only its privacy. "It's very nice as it is; thank you for the offer."

"I won't bore you with a tour of the house. As I said, I will be gone for a few days. Start tomorrow and you can use my absence to familiarize yourself with it. I am certain you would rather do it at your leisure."

She did not have to ask, it was obvious he had concluded his conversation with her, and she was now dismissed. She did not know what to make of him. There was not anything objectionable to his character, but he made a point of keeping his distance. He gave every impression he expected the same of her. The employment agency suggested as much when they first told her about the job. She recognized it was likely off putting to her predecessors and that is why they left. Where they may have been offended by his demeanor, Nora appreciated it.

"Thank you for the opportunity to work for you and I promise to give you my very best effort," she said as she extended her hand.

"I have no doubt you will." She thought she detected a sigh of relief from him. The agency did not disclose how many housekeepers he replaced. Hopefully, her employment would satisfy them both.

Nora returned to her car to process her interview. She was astonished by its brevity. Three days ago, she was driving nowhere. Now, she had both a job and a place to live. She did not have any expectations for her future self, and she did not need them. She was grateful for a chance to be anonymous, safe, and hopefully valued. She drove back to the motel office to inform Ruth of her plans.

"I guess I'll be checking out tomorrow morning." She fumbled for her credit card after she told Ruth she was leaving.

"Already?"

"Here, but not the town. I found a job and it includes lodging."

"Good for you," Ruth said in a chipper voice. "I hope we will be running into you. If you do not mind, may I ask where you will be working?"

"I will be a live-in cook and housekeeper for Benjamin Stafford. Do you know him?"

"No, I don't, but I'm familiar with his firm. I have seen it advertised and I know him to be civic minded. He generously donates to charities and local concerns. I think you will be happy working for him, at least I've never heard anyone say a word against him."

"That's good to know. I want to thank you for your hospitality."

"That's what we're in business for. Good luck to you."

She settled her bill and Ruth printed out a receipt. Nora smiled and felt her first sense of excitement at starting a new chapter in her life. She thought she would be somewhat anxious, but she slept better than she had in months. The knowledge she had a couple of days to acclimate before her new boss returned took enormous pressure off her.

The next morning, she packed her bags and headed off to start her new life. She did her level best to think only in the moment, not of the past and certainly not the future. It might prove difficult, but she was determined to make the effort.

She parked at the back of the house near the

garage. She had forgotten to ask him where to park her car, but his absence made it irrelevant. She pulled out the instructions he gave her; she did not want to mess up the security code. When she read the numbers, she snickered. "They are the same as the address to the house. It's the first thing a burglar would try." At least she wasn't going to forget it. Fortunately, everything went off without a hitch. The police or security people did not beat down the door. She made certain she locked the house after she entered. First, she double checked the lock to assure herself it didn't self lock if she stepped outside. She did not need to be embarrassed on her first day.

Her initial order of business was to unpack and organize her room. It was to be the only sanctuary she had, and she wanted to be comfortable in it. Once she was satisfied, she started to explore her new domain. As she wandered around, she was feeling like a voyeur even though it was necessary for her to learn every inch of the house. She started with the kitchen; it was adjacent to her bedroom. It was not as large as the one at the inn, but it was more efficient for a homeowner. It was equipped with a commercial style stove which pleased her, and plenty of freezer and refrigeration space. She opened them and found them woefully empty. It was the first thing she wanted to rectify before Mr. Stafford returned. The butler's pantry was a pleasant surprise. It had every small appliance and amenity she wished for to make cooking easier and efficient. She was not pleased with the cutlery. She pulled a knife from its block and ran her finger across the blade. It was dangerously dull; it instantly told her any person who preceded her was not a trained cook let alone a chef. She added it to her list of things to do. The hardware store, where Mr. Stafford had his account, likely had the resources to sharpen them.

As she headed for her next logical destination, the dining room, she passed by a small sunroom which caught her attention. It overlooked the backyard gardens vibrant in their beauty. Shrubs and flowers were in various stages of bloom with bees buzzing from one blossom to the next. Someone took great care of them. The room itself appeared unused. It held a small table with four chairs and less than comfortable looking wicker chairs. She sat in one and without cushions, they were awful; no wonder the room saw little use. The dining room was different. Everything about it was high end and very formal. Unfortunately, it was dark and uninviting from its heavy mahogany furniture to its window treatments. She passed through the main foyer to a music room. A Steinway grand piano was its main focal point, but there were other instruments as well. A violin, harp and what was oddly placed, a guitar. Nora played the piano and did not resist sitting down and trying out the magnificent instrument. Sadly, it was horrendously out of tune. She must have it tuned, not for her benefit but for the piano's sake. A piano untuned for extended periods made it difficult to retune. She appreciated its splendor too much to let it be neglected.

Next, she meandered into the main living room. It too was expensively furnished, but it lacked warmth and charm. She stood in the center of the room trying to figure out why it seemed uninviting; at the inn, the ambiance was everything. She decided to address her concerns after she had explored the entire house.

Her last stop on the main floor was Mr. Stafford's library. This was the only room she entered she understood. If the house had a heart, it was here. It too, was a bit stuffy and dark, but it had its own energy. She was a voracious reader and Mr. Stafford owned well-worn copies of all the literary classics. They were eclectically interspersed with modern politically relevant topics and fiscal interests. His desk was a history lesson. It was a large hand carved, incredibly old and worn piece. She guessed it may have had family or historical significance. Tucked away in the corner was an oversized leather chair and ottoman with a reading lamp centered on an end table. All had extensive wear. Her impression was the same as that of the desk; it was important to him, she just did not know why, and it did not matter.

A television and stereo system did not appear to be the center of anything in the room. She assumed her employer was not a TV enthusiast. She opened a cabinet at the end of the room and found an expensively stocked bar. There were bourbons and scotch, she knew from her experience at the inn were costly. They were nearly empty with replacement bottles. She discerned her boss liked his liquor.

She returned to the foyer where the light from the leaded front door sparkled on the marble tile floor. She remembered Katherine Holder said her predecessors felt like the house was a mausoleum. The rainbow of colors from the sun passing through the glass brought life to the house not death. It was welcoming. She gazed up the grand staircase and made her way to the bedrooms. One was much the same as the next. Each had its own bathroom; nice but nothing special.

When she entered his bedroom, she gasped. This man, whom she came to know through her brief contact and inspection of his house, was not in character with the room. It was dark from heavy curtains, the bed was disheveled, and clothes scattered on the floor and chairs. Her nose crinkled as she inhaled the stale air. Almost afraid to enter his bathroom, and with compelling reasons, she decided it looked like it had not been touched in months. Did her predecessors consider it sacred and avoided it? If it looked like this, no wonder. She originally thought stocking the kitchen was her priority, but no longer. This must have been the one place this organized, self-contained man let himself go. Surprisingly, it did not disturb her, it made her realize he was as human as everyone else.

He told her nothing was off limits; she took him at his word and began to shovel her way through. It was late afternoon by the time she finished her tour and making notes of what needed to be done. She relaxed the rest of the day. She needed to brace herself to start fresh in the morning, in the meantime she examined her new room. She arranged and rearranged the meagre belongings she brought with her. She thought how strange it felt not being tied down to a place or possessions. There may come a time when she missed that, but for now it was emotionally freeing.

She gazed out her sitting room window, taking in the lovely sight of the grounds. She spotted a baby rabbit nibbling on tender green clover interspersed with the otherwise perfect lawn. It seemed content with its simple life; she too wanted to feel the same. Tomorrow began her journey toward that goal.

Chapter Three

The following morning Nora woke up to the sun shining through the bedroom window. She stretched out her arms and legs before stepping to the floor. She was smiling and humming to herself as she showered and dressed. The rabbit from yesterday must have passed his contentment onto her because she felt calm and energized. The anonymity and security of her new life suited her. She'd have the opportunity to use her skills from the inn and do what she did best—cook. The salary she'd receive in the coming months was more than generous, especially since it included room and board. Keenly aware a job at a commercial restaurant paid more, she felt the demands far outweighed the rewards. She did not need the stress. She wanted an uncomplicated new life not a professional challenge. Mr. Stafford set the tone of impersonal interaction and she intended to live by it.

A bowl of cereal sufficed for breakfast; she wanted to get started on her new duties. The very first thing she did was open every window in the house as it was in desperate need of a good airing. Fortunately, the summer weather was dry and windy; exactly what she needed to clear the air in Mr. Stafford's bedroom. She stood in the doorway of his room, hands on her hips while biting her lip. "Everything must go."

She started by picking up the dirty clothes and

throwing them into two large laundry baskets. There were so many she had to stuff them in. She slid the baskets into the hall and out of her way. Then she removed anything which required drycleaning. There were several suits; the curtains and bedspread required the same treatment. She intended on taking them to the cleaners later. She placed them in a pile next to the laundry baskets outside his bedroom. She found a couple of whiskey glasses on his nightstand. This worried her; she hoped he did not have a drinking problem. There was also another one in the walk-in closet which still had a small amount of residue in it. She could smell the scotch. As she picked it up, she noticed a door which escaped her earlier inspection. She opened it and a staircase led to the attic. She thought it was an awkward spot for it to be placed but checking out a storage area was at the bottom of her list.

Once all the dirty clothes were removed, organizing the walk-in closet only took her twenty minutes. She put his shirts, suits, pants, and shoes in order by color and style, but the bathroom was another matter. Every inch of the room had to be scrubbed down from the mold in the tile grout, to the grimy floors. It promised to be an all-day job to match her standards.

She needed energizing and grabbed one of the baskets of dirty clothes as she headed for the laundry room. She stopped only long enough to make a strong pot of coffee. As it brewed, she grabbed the vacuum and cleaning supplies. She placed them in the hallway at the bottom of the stairs and carried them up as she needed them. As she carried the second basket down the stairs, she stopped dead in her tracks, and let out a shriek. The basket tipped out of her hands then rolled down the stairs, its contents spilling in all directions.

A man was standing in the foyer. He quickly put both of his hands in the air in a surrender gesture dangling a key from his finger. "I'm sorry I didn't ring the bell," he said apologetically. "I'm Brian McNair, Ben's friend. He asked me to check on you and see if you needed anything."

Her hand went to her chest. "A defibrillator would be good. You just took ten years off my life. Does anyone else have a key?"

He chuckled. "Not as far as I know. I'll ring the bell if I come again."

"Your name was on the list of things I might need to know," she panted.

In a gentlemanly fashion he picked up the laundry basket and started throwing the clothes back into it. "That's all right. I'll get it," she told him. "I just made a pot of coffee. Would you want a cup?"

"That sounds great." Leaving Nora the impression he was checking up on her to report back to his friend, he followed her into the kitchen and grabbed two coffee mugs while she tossed the basket into the laundry room.

"It looks like you know your way around here better than I do," she said.

He filled their cups with the aromatic brew and handed one to her. "I should, I lived here after my wife kicked me out of the house."

"I'm sorry," she said not knowing how to respond to this stranger.

He had a mischievous glint in his eyes. "No big deal. She and I are still friends. What about you? You divorced?"

She was instantly uncomfortable. "No."

"Do you think you'll like it here?" he asked.

She glanced around. "What's not to like?"

"Ben is a great guy," he said. "I know he seems a little aloof, maybe even odd, but he is one of the kindest people you will ever meet. He needs someone to give this house a feeling of a home."

She was hesitant but asked, "Is there anything I need to know to make his life easier? He is paying me well and I do not want to disappoint him."

Mr. McNair twirled his coffee mug in his hand before taking another sip. "He isn't hard to please, but he is a very private person. Apart from an occasional round of golf with me, he doesn't go out much."

Recognizing his obvious devotion to his friend, Nora smiled. "You really like him."

He nodded. "Yeah. We were college roommates. We did everything together and he kept me out of countless messy situations. His parents and sister became my family. I love them all dearly; you will too."

"Are you in the same line of work?"

His lips slipped into a cockeyed position and his eyes sparkled with humor. "No, and don't hold it against me, but I'm a lawyer."

"I try not to judge," she told him trying to be as relaxed as he was, but it did not come naturally.

"I have an office near Ben's building. We often meet up for lunch."

"What area of law do you practice?" she asked, not prying, but rather to be polite in conversation.

"I guess you might say I have a general practice. I

do a little of this and that. I avoid criminal law; there are other lawyers in my office who take on those cases. I excel, if I do say so myself, at estate planning and business law." He took a final slurp of his coffee. "Well, I'll let you get back to your chores. Call me if you need anything."

She walked him to the door. "Oh, I forgot to tell you the main reason I stopped by; Ben has to stay another day, so he won't be home tomorrow."

She nodded and locked the door behind him when he left. She was relieved Mr. Stafford's stay was extended an extra day because she wanted everything perfect. She did not plan for the entire day it was taking to clean his bedroom. She worked well into the evening stopping only long enough to run to the drycleaner. By the end of the day, the room sparkled, and she was pleased. She only hoped Mr. Stafford thought so.

****.

The next morning, she began with her original priority, the kitchen. She made a meticulous list of what she felt was needed, and it was considerable. He told her having a cook was paramount. She knew exactly what a well-equipped kitchen needed, and it was a waste of time and money when it was not. She checked the list he left her and went to the grocery store where he had an account. She was overwhelmed by the scope of the supermarket. In the small town of Darling where she had lived, there was nothing to compare. When she wanted specialty items, she frequented several different stores, but here everything she wanted was at her fingertips. There was no necessity for her to seek a butcher shop or seafood store; the grocery store had the best of everything. She preferred to buy meats and poultry as she needed them to ensure their freshness, but fruits and vegetables kept for days. She filled the largest grocery cart to the brim; the bill ran to more than three-hundred dollars. Not everything she bought was to be used at once. Many items, such as spices, did not need to be replaced with any frequency. She preferred fresh spices when seasonably available but used dry herbs in a pinch.

What a blessed relief and distraction it was to her to be able to reorganize and fill the kitchen pantry. She'd not had a single moment of homesickness, nor was she distracted by negative thoughts. Nora was in her element as she wiped down the luxurious granite countertops and put a shine on the stainless-steel appliances. Taking a prideful moment to appreciate her accomplishments she realized she had time to finish the rest of the house which only needed a little dusting and vacuuming. She wanted to take extra care in his library. He explicitly told her it was the most important room in the house. She made certain not to move anything out of its original spot as she polished and cleaned. On one bookcase there was a photograph of Mr. Stafford's college graduation; she knew this because his friend Brian McNair stood next to him. The graduation date displayed confirmed her assumption of his age. He would now be in his forties. The men easily passed for brothers despite Brian's distinctive red hair. She realized it was the only photograph she had seen in the entire house, in fact, there were very few personal items anywhere. The house lacked personalization and it felt as though it had been stripped of its heart, leaving only an attractive shell. While she thought about it, she realized the same was true of herself. She brought nothing with her except clothing and a couple of mementos. Marjorie was kind enough to let her store her possessions in the basement of the inn until she decided what she wanted to do with her life. She felt unencumbered, leaving everything behind, at least for now. She wondered if Mr. Stafford was doing the same thing, only he stayed in one spot.

Confident she was earning her paycheck, everything in the house had been brought up to her standards and those were the hardest ones to achieve. Though ready for Mr. Stafford's return, she was becoming a little uneasy about having him in the house. During the time he'd been gone, she'd not been accountable to anyone and worried about her self-imposed exile being disrupted. However, she was determined to make this position work.

She took the liberty of buying one thing for herself at the grocery store and that was a box of her favorite tea. She made herself a cup and sat down to relax in the sunroom. Nora thought it was the most pleasant room in the house. It was bright and airy, unlike the rest of the house, which had an oppressive feeling. It suddenly occurred to her the only place she had not gone was outside. There was a beautiful flagstone patio, and the warm summer day was made more pleasant by the sun starting to fade into dusk. She took her cup of tea with her as she walked outside. It was a unique neighborhood because all the houses in the cul-de-sac were built on three acre lots. It was an extreme amount of space for a suburban home, but the homes were built prior to the popularity of living outside the city. She envisioned it as a farm which had been parceled into building lots to maximize its value. The trees and shrubs were fully mature, and she could barely see into anyone's yard. The inn enjoyed an extra-large lot in the village but with no comparison to this stately neighborhood minutes from a large city. She detected the sound of water running and headed further into the yard. She strolled down a winding brick walkway in its direction. It led to a fountain surrounded by a colorful flower garden. It was meticulous in its planning and maintenance with copious shrubs and flowers. It was as lovely as any park she had ever walked through. A bench near the fountain invited her to sit. As she surveyed her surroundings, she saw a small marker next to a flowering rosebush. She bent to read it. "No flower so beautiful, no sun so bright or riches so great which could replace you in my heart."

How sad. What must he have lost? She knew, all too well, about loss. She wondered if this was a tribute or a painful reminder. Her own pain kept her from being curious enough to find out.

She went back to the house just in time to hear a sound she had not heard before in the days living in the house—the ringing of the landline. She darted to grab it before the answering machine picked it up. "Stafford residence."

"Nora, this is Ben Stafford. I will be home around four in the afternoon tomorrow if my plane is on time." He never asked how she was making out or if there were any problems.

"I will be expecting you. Is there anything you want done before your return?"

He paused. "No, I can't think of anything, but I will be home for dinner. Did any packages or mail arrive for me?"

"No packages, but I placed the mail on your desk in the library as you instructed."

"Thank you. I'll see you tomorrow."

She placed the phone back on the receiver. "Tomorrow will tell if this is the right place for me."

Chapter Four

Nora wanted the first meal she prepared for Mr. Stafford to be special, because she felt it set the tone for future dinners. While she looked for cookbooks or recipes in the kitchen, she found a small notebook kept by her predecessors. It held valuable information about his preferences. It described how he liked his meat cooked, desired side dishes, desserts, and even wine choices. There was a notation to always have branch water on hand. Patrons of the inn often requested branch water when they ordered bourbon. It explained the preference for his ample bourbon supply. This gave her an insight which may have taken her days, even weeks to have learned on her own.

She spent the entire day on menu planning, a preparation which was ironically more difficult to cook for one than a group. She was clever about preserving and reusing leftovers so if she prepared too much, she would not waste a thing. When she ran the inn, it was important to plan carefully. The budget was tight, and waste was the enemy. The day flew by as it always did when she was cooking. When a few minutes past four o'clock, she heard his car in the driveway. She did not go to greet him. She let him seek her if he wanted something. She was at his disposal not the other way around.

****

Ben Stafford unlocked the front door, stepped inside, and set his suitcase down taking in his surroundings. Everything was as he'd left it, but somehow it was different. He was not able to put his finger on it, but it felt changed. The house had a lighter feeling. He promptly took his things upstairs to his bedroom. When he entered, he was so dumbstruck he dropped his suitcase and said aloud, "Holy s...," not finishing the word. The five-star hotel he just left was not as nice as his own room. His nostrils were assailed with the scent of disinfectant. He peeked into the bathroom. The towels were folded and hung in order of size, the soap was replenished and even the toilet paper was folded in a neat triangle. His further inspection of the closet was no less impressive. He was almost afraid to touch anything. For the first time in years, he carefully unpacked his bag, hung up his clothes, and threw the dirty ones into a conveniently accessible hamper. He changed into casual wear before heading to the library.

Sometimes this house felt like his prison and other times his sanctuary. Today it felt good to be home. As he sat down at his desk to go over the mail, he smiled with appreciation, at the plate of hors d'oeuves and a tall bourbon with branch water. He lifted the glass, swirled the ice cubes, and closed his eyes as he took a sip. Nothing ever tasted so good.

He flipped through his mail with most of it ending up in the wastebasket. He found the envelope of money he'd given her with only the amount missing for the hardware store with the receipt inside. She left the receipt from the grocery store. As he scanned the receipt his head shot back, and his eyes widened. Its total was unexpected, but he did not doubt the purchases were necessary. His refrigerator was woefully empty when he left. Previous cooks were average at best and from the items on the bill he had higher hopes for Nora's efforts. She did not disappoint him. He was not certain why a cook was so important to him when he had such simple needs, but he liked the idea of not eating out. He detested preparing his own meals and had no interest in learning to cook.

****

Nora did not bother her new employer. She had plenty to do preparing dinner and if he wanted something, he knew where to find her. She went into the dining room and set the table. Not knowing what his preferences were, if he even had any, she placed a linen tablecloth on the table. She used the fine China and silverware, complemented by imported crystal glasses. It looked beautiful but lonely with such a huge table and only one setting. She never compared it to herself because she sat at the kitchen island for her meal. It did not seem to have the same meaning, yet they were both alone.

He told her he preferred to dine at seven, so at precisely seven she had his meal ready. When she entered his library, she had her first face to face meeting with him since she was hired. She knocked gently on the woodwork as he looked up from his desk. "Welcome home, sir. Dinner is ready in the dining room."

He picked up his hors d'oeuvre plate and glass. "Thank you, Nora. The appetizers were appreciated."

She took the dishes from him and went to the kitchen as he sat down at the massive dining room table. She peered at him from the kitchen, and he seemed slightly perplexed at the formality of his place setting. She wondered if his earlier employees had served him in the same manner. He picked up a crystal water goblet, examined it as if he had never seen it before, and took a sip from it. He shrugged and smiled. Her question was answered; her predecessors did not have her attention to detail.

Nora remembered the words of the employment agency manager telling her he did not like to interact with his housekeepers. She kept her distance while maintaining a professional eye on his dining needs. The formality was comforting for her. She took the approach of not speaking unless directly engaged. He showed every sign he was of a similar mind and shared her formal interactions.

She placed fresh baked rolls with butter in a basket next to his plate, a wine goblet was yet to be filled. The fragrant roll was the first thing he grabbed, slathering it with butter. Nora entered the room with a cup of beef mushroom soup and a spinach salad. She placed them before him, he thanked her when she returned with the wine. She presented him with the bottle. "I'm not sure what you prefer but I took the liberty of pairing it with the meal. It was among your wine collection, I deduced it was something you enjoyed."

He practically stuttered when he told her it was acceptable and motioned for her to pour. She watched him to gauge when to bring in the main course. After a suitable amount of time, she served a lobster stuffed salmon with fresh asparagus on a silver platter. Again, he thanked her, but his pace of consumption had slowed. She was aware the meal may have been too elaborate, but she needed to display her skills. Cooking was a panacea to all her troubles, and she hoped Mr. Stafford took the same pleasure in dining. It was, after all, her primary job. When he finished his meal, she came in to clear the plates and asked, "Would you care for dessert?"

He groaned and patted his stomach to show he was full. Curiosity got the better of him. "What did you make?"

"I haven't actually made it yet. It was going to be a simple peach flambé. I intended to prepare it here at the table."

In a profoundly serious tone he asked, "Do you intend to cook like this every night?"

She was afraid he was displeased. "Unless you tell me otherwise."

He lifted his plate for her to take. "I would be insane to do that, but I honestly did not have this high of an expectation. The employment agency was aware of my priority in having a cook; I never imagined this. I have dined at Michelin star restaurants whose meals can't compare to yours."

"You want me to tone it down?" she asked hurt that her culinary efforts may not be appreciated.

He was quick to reassure her. "If you enjoy it, I will certainly take every advantage, but don't think this is always necessary. I was raised on a simpler fare; I am content with a hot nutritious meal."

What he did not know was Nora had no life beyond her position with him, so whether she made a ten-course meal or a sandwich, she was going to give it her entire attention.

"Is that a *no* on the dessert?" She smiled.

He was quiet for a moment. "Oh, what the heck; go for it."

She laughed to herself as she went to the kitchen to get the flambé pan and ingredients. Men loved desserts and often mistook a woman's ability to cook with baking. Nora was proficient at both; however, given a preference she chose cooking. She prided herself on her ability to turn the most meager of ingredients into a fine dinner.

It was after eight o'clock by the time Mr. Stafford finished his dinner and she found herself exhausted, but happily so. As she was cleaning up the kitchen he entered. "As much as I was looking forward to what you may cook tomorrow morning, I have a breakfast meeting. Just have the coffee ready for me."

Then he started to walk from the room when he stopped and turned back to face her. "About my bedroom, it will never look like the way I left it again."

Nora laughed aloud and it felt good. "I can guarantee it."

He bit his lip and smiled. "I think you can."

Nora retired to her room exhausted, more mentally than physically. At least she felt he was genuinely pleased. Finding any kind of a new routine was daunting. It would have surprised her to learn Ben had similar feelings. The reason his other housekeepers never lasted was simple—they did not seem to fit in. He and Nora unknowingly shared an inexplicable kinship. She was effortless in her competency and instincts, and he was receptive to them.

She rose early the next morning not knowing what time he wanted his coffee she waited until seven to brew it, insuring its freshness. She grabbed the morning paper which had been thrown near the front door and placed it on the kitchen island. When Mr. Stafford came in for his coffee, she asked, "It's a beautiful morning; perhaps you would prefer to take your coffee on the terrace with your paper?"

He looked out the kitchen window at the patio furniture. "I'd enjoy that."

She poured the coffee into an insulated carafe, placed it on a tray with a large mug, coffee creamer, and sugar. She positioned it before him on a glass coffee table to allow him to serve himself.

****

Ben watched as Nora returned to the house. He felt awkward being catered to so diligently, but he found himself enjoying every moment of it. More than just her meticulous attention to detail, he discovered she had the ability to make him appreciate what he had by drawing attention to it. He loved his gardens. It was he who designed them and lovingly planted each flower and shrub. It was his one true passion. The lawn he left to a service; excepting the spring and fall clean-up, he did everything himself. He was disappointed he spent more time working on the gardens than enjoying them. He was determined to change that as he leaned back in his patio chair. He closed his eyes and took in the scents and sounds around him.

****

Making it a point of being as observant as possible, Nora watched her new employer from the window. He was clearly content as he read his newspaper and drank his coffee. After he had left for the office, she began her daily routine. She tidied up his bedroom and office, lightly dusted and vacuumed, and most importantly, planned his meals. As she checked her recipes and ingredients something caught her eye. A bright red cardinal was sitting on the outside windowsill of the sunroom. She stepped closer to watch when she spotted a nest deep inside a nearby bush. She did not want to frighten it and backed up. When she did, she knocked over a small chair. It caused her to take a discerning look around the room.

"What a waste," she said aloud, remembering Mr. Stafford gave her free rein except for his office. She decided to rearrange the furnishings. She slid the small table with its four chairs to the center of the bay window where the bird had perched. She then made a seating arrangement at the opposite side of the room with the remaining chairs and end tables. She vaguely recalled seeing scattered household items in the basement next to Mr. Stafford's wine racks. There were cushions to make the chairs more comfortable and an unattractive but colorful rug. She dragged them up and took them outside to freshen them from the musty cellar and was pleased with the result. The room now had a purpose for informal dining. She did not know how her boss might feel about it, but he seemed so lost in the dining room by himself. He looked uneasy with the formality of the dining room; she hoped he might appreciate a change.

She set the sunroom table with the same formality, but the ambiance was strikingly different. When he returned from the office, she continued the practice of having his bourbon and light hors d'oeuvres placed at his desk. However, when she informed him that his dinner was ready, she escorted him to the sunroom. "I took the liberty of serving your dinner here. If you have an objection, I certainly will not have the audacity to do it again."

He stood in the entrance of the room looking around. In a quiet, almost reverent voice he said, "I have always had a fondness for this room. It just never quite suited me despite its ideal view of the gardens. It hadn't occurred to me to turn it into a dining space. I can imagine it being just as beautiful in the winter."

He turned to look at her eagerness for his approval. "Thank you. I never felt relaxed in the dining room except of course when I was entertaining. This is perfect."

She said nothing before going back to the order of business, which was serving his dinner. He seldom let his eyes divert from the view of the garden. It gave Nora an insight into him. The simplicity of a sparsely decorated room with an enchanting view meant more than the grandeur of his dining room. She brought out his dessert of fresh berries in sherried cream and watched as he spooned them into his mouth, never taking his eyes off the garden. "Thank you."

She sensed he wanted to say more but he did not. "It is my pleasure, sir."

He shook his head. "No, I mean I really thank you. This is now my new favorite room. You are an artist not just a chef. I appreciate your talent."

He then fell silent. This had become their lives. Seldom was it necessary for either to exchange more than a few words. What was not obvious to either of them was the volumes they were speaking in that silence.

Nora never thought about whether she was happy or not. That was not even a priority, but she liked knowing when Ben was home. When he had gone on an occasional business trip the house seemed empty despite the fact they seldom indulged in discourse. Ben had his business associates and his friendship with Brian McNair for companionship. All Nora had was a passing acquaintance with the butcher; still, it had been enough, but she felt a twinge of selfishness. She wanted to give of herself to help others. One morning while serving Ben his breakfast she asked, "Sir, may I discuss something with you?"

Ben dropped his newspaper. His eyebrows furrowed and his voice was unsteady as if he were expecting unwelcome news. "Certainly."

"I read in the newspaper the local Veteran's Hospital is in desperate need of volunteers. If I can assure you it will not interfere with my duties here, may I help out a few hours a couple times a week?"

"Good heavens, Nora!" he exclaimed with such passion she thought he was angry. "You have been here for weeks and never taken a single day off. I am embarrassed I haven't insisted you get out more. Of course, you can and do anything else you like. See a movie, get a manicure; anything."

She looked at her nails with a smirk. "Do they look that bad?"

He laughed. "No, they are perfect, but seriously you do not need my permission for anything. If I need you here at a specific time for some reason, I will let you know in advance. I would hate for you to be cooped up here day in and day out. I am certain you need a life outside these four walls."

She wanted to tell him she did not want a life outside the four walls. She was perfectly content with things the way they were, but her conscience did not allow her that luxury. "Thank you, Mr. Stafford," she said, thus completing the longest conversation they had ever exchanged.

Chapter Five

The next morning after Ben left for work, Nora set out for the Veteran's Hospital. It was on the outskirts of town at the edge of the city limits. She easily found it but was taken aback as she approached the parking garage. It appeared brand new nestled on the edge of a golf course which she later learned also belonged to the hospital. In addition to the hospital, it had an attached nursing home for disabled veterans who were no longer capable of living independently. She had previously volunteered at a Veteran's Hospital near her hometown, but it was shamefully inadequate and in no comparison to the one she now entered.

On her way to the office of volunteers, she passed patients with varying degrees of medical issues. She was not deterred; she had seen it all before. There were soldiers—men and women with missing limbs, blind, severely burned, and mentally incapacitated. The administration was more than happy for her help.

A retired army captain oversaw the volunteer program. He read her application and said, "I see you have volunteered at our northern Pennsylvania hospital."

Nora nodded.

"That is always a plus," he said. "There are well intentioned people who want to help, but they have no idea what to expect. Approximately a third of the volunteers who come to the hospital last only a few visits. Their efforts are greatly appreciated, but they were not equipped to deal directly with the patients. Of course, there are other functions they might perform. What did you do at the hospital?"

She told him she read newspapers, books, and magazines to the patients, but mostly they just wanted someone to listen to them. It was the greatest gift she possessed, her ability to listen. It did not seem to matter which war they fought in; the people were the same just on different battlefields. She heard stories of heroism, cowardice, fear, loneliness, and despair. There were also comedic moments usually used to distract from the terror they faced daily. Sadly, there were also those who had lost touch with reality. Their minds flowed in and out of coherency and it broke her heart.

He smiled but had a mournful look on his face. "Then you know what to expect."

Again, she nodded. She had wished she did not know, but she knew only too well. She liked to think the time spent with the soldiers was a testament to her character, but she knew better. She was not volunteering because she took as much from them as they did her. She volunteered purely because it was the right thing to do. She wanted to give back to them, in some small measure, what they had sacrificed for her. It was a difficult thing for her to do. If she wanted only to be charitable, there were other organizations she might choose from. She loved animals; shelters everywhere needed volunteers. She might lend a hand at the soup kitchen, which was her expertise, or even aid with community fund raisers. Everything was less demanding of her than the Veteran's Hospital, but it was where she belonged.

Nora gave the captain a schedule conducive to her hours at Mr. Stafford's' home. She was not committed to being there at those hours, but she honored the commitment she made. If Mr. Stafford needed her, it took priority, but he was more than flexible. As she was leaving for home, she walked down a corridor of exam rooms when a pregnant young woman came from one of the offices. "Hi. Did you find a job?"

Nora gave her a confused look. How did this woman know her, but then she recognized her from the restaurant. "You are the waitress who told me to call the employment agency. Yes, I did, and I am very happily employed," she replied surprised the woman remembered her. "Are you in the military?"

She patted her enlarged stomach. "No, my husband is. He is doing a tour in the Middle East. We have hopes he will be back by the time the baby arrives. It is our first."

Nora said a quick prayer in her head for his safety. The world did not need another fatherless child. "I wish you all the best. I am volunteering here so maybe we'll see each other again. I'm Nora."

"Christa," she said shaking her hand.

****

Brian called Ben to invite him for a game of golf. They met at the country club in the early afternoon. Brian was nearly obsessed with golf and a far better player, but he enjoyed Ben's company. They spoke of only inconsequential things like politics, sports, and the weather. It was pointless for Brian to expect any intimate details from Ben. His friend had been leading such a solitary life for the past few years he was aware little had changed, except of course, his new housekeeper. It was on that point he prodded Ben. "How is Nora working out?"

It was with the most enthusiasm he had seen from his friend in a long time when Ben answered, "Great. I couldn't have found someone more perfect if I searched the globe. It's like having an invisible mind reader in the house. If I want a drink, it appears; if I am hungry, a plate of food is just there. I drop something on the floor, it's put back. Her culinary skills would rival any high-end restaurant."

"I'm happy you finally found someone to stay," he said, "but what's her story?"

"What do you mean?"

"I only met her for a few minutes, but even I can tell she was running or hiding from something."

Ben's brow furrowed. "What makes you say that?"

"If what you have said about her is true, why is she working for you?"

"Thanks a lot."

"I don't mean you're not a nice guy, but why wouldn't she go to some place where her talents can be appreciated? What do you really know about her?"

Ben leaned in toward Brian. "I know she is darn good at what she does. She has been honest and reliable. What more do I need to know? Stop looking for problems where none exist."

His almost passionate defense of her prompted Brian to say, "I'm not casting aspersions on her. For what little contact I had with her I like her. I didn't see any red flags; she was pleasant but impersonally polite."

Brian had been Ben's rock through tough times and

unfailingly loyal. If he raised any concerns about Nora, it was only in the protection of his friend. The fact that she kept her distance from everyone was a good sign she had no ulterior motives beyond her job. If she were trying to play Ben for a fool for his money, she would do everything in her power to ingratiate herself to him, not be aloof.

Brian held up a hand to stop Ben from saying anything further. "I'm just saying, there is a story there someplace. Maybe an ex-husband or lost love."

"That's her business not mine. Why don't you come for dinner on Saturday? You can interrogate her if you like."

"I think I will do that very thing."

****

Ben was not sure if he was being protective of Nora's reputation or protective of the comfortable life he had come to know. The truth fell somewhere in the middle. He did not want to think he had bad judgment and he did not want to hear anything negative about someone he respected. Whatever the reason might be, they comfortably coexisted.

He arrived home a little earlier than usual and went directly to the kitchen to find Nora. She was peeling vegetables when she looked up. "I wasn't expecting you so soon. I am sorry I don't have your refreshments ready."

Brian's comments had made him slightly paranoid, so he was relieved to find her doing just what he had expected. "That's okay; I was playing golf with Mr. McNair, and we shared an appetizer. I invited him to dinner on Saturday. Don't go all out; there is nothing he'd rather have than a thick charcoal grilled steak and a cold beer. In fact, we will eat al fresco if it doesn't rain."

"Sounds simple enough," she said pleasantly never taking her attention off the vegetables.

He started to leave and then turned back. "Did you go to the hospital today?"

She nodded. "Yes, it is a very impressive place. Not like others I have visited."

"Oh, you've done this before?" He had believed she was new to volunteering.

She did not go into details, she simply replied, "I like to do what I can for our veterans."

"I admire that. There is a charity my firm sponsors. We give where and how we can."

The subject ended and he went out to the garden to work before dinner. It was a place which brought him complete reverie. There he cultivated the color and vibrancy his life lacked.

****

Nora did not want to disappoint Mr. Stafford so she did not tell him barbequing was not her forte. She had already proven her acumen in the kitchen but wrestling with a grill was another matter. She remembered what her father told her about starting the charcoal early and letting it slowly burn down. She trusted he was right. She took Mr. Stafford's promise his friend had simple tastes. She thought the side dishes and presentation better be sufficient to cover for a bad steak.

On Saturday she carried a large tub up from the basement and filled it with ice, beer, and bottled water then placed it in the shade on the patio. She didn't notice his guest had arrived. He came through the garden and was making himself at home with a beer he grabbed when Ben came in from the back part of the lawn.

"Hey," Brian yelled to him. "It's too hot to slave in the yard."

Ben laughed; a sound Nora seldom heard from him. He was usually so serious and staid.

"How would you know? I don't think you've ever gotten your hands dirty in your life," Ben replied lightly as he washed up at the garden sink.

"That's why I live in a townhouse—no maintenance."

"No soul either," Ben said looking lovingly onto his garden.

As she listened to their jovial exchange, Nora took a tray of cheese and crackers along with two iced beer mugs and went outside. As she set them down, Brian stood. "Nice to see you again, Nora."

There was something infectiously amiable about him. "It's good to see you again too, Mr. McNair."

"Don't be so formal," he began as he sat back down. "Call me Brian. Why don't you grab a cold one and join us?"

Ben shot him a disapproving look. Not that he was likely to have any objections to her having a beer, but they had carefully constructed a formal relationship. Brian had inadvertently crossed the line. It made her uncomfortable, so she diplomatically responded, "Thank you, sir, but I have several things I'm in the middle of in the kitchen."

****

"What are you doing?" Ben said aghast. "You're a guest; she works for me."

Opening another beer, he said, "She's not an

indentured servant, for goodness sake. Lighten up."

Ben whispered but his words were distinct. "Would you ask a waitress at a restaurant to join you?"

He popped a cube of cheese into his mouth. "I've done that."

Ben just shook his head and laughed. "Hence your divorce. Just knock off your crap when you are around her. Do not screw this up for me."

Ben relaxed because Brian behaved himself and did not goad him or impose himself on Nora any further. Despite his childish behavior, he trusted Brian to be a gentleman. He had an easy manner which magnetically drew people to him, unfortunately it was sometimes his downfall. He was always fun to be around and loyal to a fault in his friendship. He was the brother Ben never had. The backyard was filled with laughter and back and forth bantering between the two friends. After a few beers were downed by the pair, Nora brought out the steaks and side dishes. Brian took his first bite and closed his eyes in pure rapture. "If you don't marry her, I will," he uttered over a mouthful of food.

"If it were the only way I could keep her here to do all my cooking, I think I would. Every meal she makes is spectacular. I have already put on weight."

"Forget about any suspicious remarks I may have made about her. Anyone who can make a steak like this has to be a paragon of virtue. Where's dessert?"

Ben shook his head. "You're incorrigible."

It had been a long time since Ben had just kicked back and enjoyed himself. He no longer worried about details; he relaxed but the downside was more time to brood. Brian was a break from his melancholy. Even in good times he never possessed Brian's vivacious personality. In college Ben was not an extrovert, it was one of the reasons the two were such close friends. Brian was the type of person who gleaned another's entire life history from them in a matter of minutes. He was good for Ben; he helped him become more personable even if it was forced. Brian liked to be the life of the party, have his ego stroked by women and be recognized by his peers. It made him a great attorney but a rotten husband; however, he was loyal to the bone sometimes even to his own detriment. Ben was the opposite; he shunned the limelight and was content with remaining anonymous when he performed any act of kindness. It was a characteristic Brian admired but did not emulate.

****

Unlike Ben, Nora had no Brian. She was totally on her own. It was unnecessary, but she consciously chose it. In fact, there were so many people who genuinely cared about her, it was the reason she left town. She was able to handle just about anything but kindness and pity. She worried it might deprive her of the toughness she needed to move forward. If her parents were still living, or if she had a sibling, then she may have shared her burden. She had no one to empathize with the torture her soul felt. The only person she relied on was Marjorie.

Before leaving Darling, Nora changed her cell phone number. The only person in possession of it was Marjorie, and it was for emergencies only. Mr. Stafford was the second person to have it in case he needed something when she was not at home.

She didn't take the opportunity to evaluate her

future. Angst, pain, and despair gnawed at her soul. She fled Pennsylvania to prevent being destroyed by the demons that haunted her. Nora was not a coward, that wasn't her reason for leaving. She left because she was smothered by who she became. If she took a moment to think of herself, she may have been kinder. She never treated another individual with the harsh and unrelenting lack of forgiveness she condemned herself with. She gazed out the kitchen window and smiled. She envied the loyal camaraderie her employer and his friend so obviously shared.

Ben and Brian finally finished their meal; she dutifully went outside to the patio to collect the dishes. Ben jumped to his feet. "I'll help you carry these dishes inside."

Waving him off she said, "No, you'll only interfere with my system."

Brian laughed. "She's got you there, Ben. Until now I never met anyone who was more organized than you."

Ben grinned and waved his hands in a surrender gesture. "Far be it from me to overstep my bounds."

Nora enjoyed the moment of lightness. "Would you gentleman like an after-dinner brandy?"

Ben gave her an approving nod before she headed to the house. She suppressed a giggle when she overheard Brian say, "Amazing, she really is a mind reader. Do you think she would moonlight for me?"

Ben slapped him on his leg. "I'd sooner let her work for the Marquis de Sade."

Nora returned with two snifters of brandy pretending not to hear Brian say, "Just a thought."

Chapter Six

As the days of summer waned, little changed in the lives of Nora or Ben. The absence of external forces allowed them to continue in respectful and amiable indifference. On one autumn evening all that changed. Nora was startled awake when she heard a pounding on her door. "Nora, Nora."

She instantly recognized Ben's voice. With concern, but not fear, she flung the door open. He leaned against the door jam, sweat beading down his face, and bent over holding his stomach. She placed her arm around his waist and ushered him in as she helped him sit on the sofa. He groaned, his breathing fast and uneven. "I…. I think it's my appendix."

Nora wiped his face with the sleeve of her bathrobe. She didn't need a thermometer to know he was burning with fever. "Do you want me to call an ambulance?"

He shook his head still bent over. "I don't want to wait. Can you drive me to the emergency room? It's faster."

She realized he was right, not because emergency services were far away, but because the hospital was so close. She did not answer him; she threw on her clothes, grabbed her purse and car keys. She held him up as he staggered to her car. She tried to remain calm as she watched him clutch his abdomen and the color drain from his face.

The ten-minute drive seemed like an eternity. She pulled into the ambulance bay at the emergency room door where staff instantly appeared with a wheelchair and whisked him inside. He looked small and helpless as the orderly wheeled him down the hallway, disappearing from her sight. People asked questions she was not able to answer. What insurance does he have, who is his next of kin, does he have any prior medical conditions? She was of no help, but she knew who to call, Brian. He was certain to have answers. Her hands shook as she took her cellphone from her purse. She was relieved she thought to put his number into her directory. Her voice shook as hard as her hands. "Mr. McNair, I'm at the hospital with Mr. Stafford. Please come here right away."

He was there in a matter of minutes and Nora felt relief to pass the torch to him. What did she have to contribute? Other than being a person he was acquainted with, she was of little use. She was dismayed to discover Brian was just as flustered. He burst through the emergency room entrance yelling, "Where is he? Is he all right?" He was so panicked she thought she would have to slap him.

Nora tried to keep her voice calm. "He's being examined; maybe they will take you back to see him." Her prediction was realized when a nurse said he may stay for a few moments with him. Meanwhile the emergency room receptionist asked Nora to come to the intake desk.

"I just wanted to let you know we found Mr. Stafford's insurance information. It was on file from a time when he was here for a routine physical."

Nora exhaled, releasing the tension which had built inside her. "At least you have that. I'm sorry I'm of so little help, I only started working for him recently. His friend has more information."

"That's okay. First things first and that's taking care of him," the receptionist said in a reassuring voice.

Ten minutes later Brian returned to the waiting room. "It's definitely his appendix and they're prepping him for surgery. It will be a while before we know anything. You can go home if you want, but I'd prefer to have some company if you do not mind staying with me."

She patted his arm. "I won't sleep anyway; of course, I'll stay. Is there someone we need to call?"

"When they asked him to sign the surgical consent form, he also signed a waiver for me to make medical decisions for him. It's best we wait to call anyone. His mother lives in the Carolina's and is not in the best of health; I don't want to worry her. She and Ben's father moved there when they retired. After he died six years ago, she decided to stay because the cold winters up here were more than she wanted to handle."

"Does he have a brother or sister, maybe?"

"He has a younger sister, but she and her husband live in Sweden. He is a structural engineer and his company sent them there several years ago. Ben told me they are moving back soon."

Nora's head dropped to her chest. "Doesn't sound like Mr. Stafford has much support."

Brian straightened his shoulders and stood tall. "He's got us, we're all he needs."

It was two hours before the doctor appeared from the operating room to give them an update. "He came through the surgery fine, but the appendix did rupture. Our main concern is to ensure peritonitis does not set in. I put in drains, and we'll keep a close eye on infection. He is going to be off his feet for a while."

"Can I see him?" Brian asked.

The doctor patted his shoulder. "Why don't you come back after you've gotten some rest. He will be groggy for several hours."

Both Brian and Nora were exhausted. He walked her to her car yawning as she drove off. She went home but it was the hour she normally arose anyway, so she made a pot of coffee. It had barely finished brewing when Brian knocked on the kitchen door. "You can't sleep either, huh?" he asked.

She shook her head. "There'll be time for that, I guess."

Brian helped himself to the coffee just as he had the first time they met. He was examining its contents before taking a sip. Speaking into the cup he said, "I'm glad you were here, and so is Ben."

Nora did not take credit. "He would have just called an ambulance for himself or perhaps call you."

He set his cup down and snatched a cupcake he spotted on a covered cake dish, ravishing it. "But that's not how it played out. Do you ever think people are at a place and time when they are needed?"

Before she knew it words spewed from her lips. "I do not! Terrible things happen all the time with no intervention."

His head bobbed backward. "It was just a theoretical question. I'm the last person to know."

She waved her hand and grimaced. "Sorry, I'm tired and more than a little worried about Mr. Stafford. I was thinking when he comes home, he will be in no condition to go up and down the stairs for a while. I will move my things upstairs to one of the guest rooms and he can stay in my room; that way everything will be accessible to him. Do you think he'd have any objections?"

Brian had his elbows on the countertop holding up his head, eyes drooping. "You really don't know him as I do. You look around this place and see affluence everywhere, but that's not Ben. He did not grow up poor, but not like this. It was a trap which came with his success. If it all was gone tomorrow, I honestly don't think he'd care. People matter to him, not things."

Nora admitted she knew little about her employer's personal associations, but she did know that beyond Brian she saw no other friends. "I've never seen him with anyone but you."

"How many friends do you need? I'm a lawyer, and I have dozens of friendly acquaintances. Out of them, I maybe have a half a dozen I consider close enough to sort of, depend on. I have only one devoted friend and that's Ben. He is the kind of friend I can call in the middle of the night and ask, 'can I borrow your car, a shovel, and a large trash bag' and it would be waiting for me with no questions asked. He would tell you the same thing. Even if we had not been in communication for years, that will not change. There are relationships which defy explanation."

Nora knew what he was trying to convey. Everyone thinks they are unique, that no one identifies with or feels the things they do, but it was not true. She was not unique, Brian was not unique, and neither was Ben. The only element which may be unique was their perspective or tolerance of their difficulties.

"Do you mind if I crashed here for a while?"

"It isn't up to me, but I'm sure Mr. Stafford would be more than okay with it."

Brian headed for the living room sofa while she packed up her clothing and toiletries to take to an upstairs guest room. She briefly peeked her head in when she heard snoring loud enough to shake the windows. She just laughed to herself and continued with her tasks.

Three hours later, he appeared groggy but announced, "I'm going back to the hospital. Do you want to tag along?"

"No, it's not my place. If there is anything I can do for either of you, please let me know."

"Are you sure? I think he'd at least like to thank you for driving him to the hospital. I won't stay long."

She shook her head. "There are things I need to get done here. He isn't going to be able to eat a normal diet for a while and that is the main reason he hired me. I want to make a pot of broth."

****

Brian was not fooled; he was certain she did not want to break the impersonal relationship she and Ben formed, so he went to the hospital without her. He found his friend awake but in a less than a joyous mood. "You look like something the cat dragged in."

Looking pale and weak, Ben pulled himself up. "Thanks, I can always count on you to lift my spirits."

"What did the doctors tell you?"

"It could have been worse. They want me to stay for a couple of days because they are worried about infection, but I'll live." He looked past Brian to the hallway. "Where's Nora?"

He was right; Ben wanted to thank her. "She is already preparing for you to come home. She moved out of her room, so you won't have to take the stairs for a while."

He struggled to move around in the bed. "She didn't have to do that. I'm sure I can do the stairs."

"Why take a chance when you don't have to? Now she can pretend you are the servant."

"Fat lot of good I'd do her; I'm useless."

"I didn't think you wanted me to call your mother until you were feeling better."

He slumped back down beneath the covers. "Thank God you didn't. She would have a conniption and be on the next plane. She means well, but she needs more care than I do. In a few days I will call and tell her what happened. Will you call Mark at the office and ask him to hold down the fort?"

"Not a problem. He has probably been waiting for a chance like this anyway. You know, like a coup."

Ben shot him with a look of disdain. "Very funny, you know he can run the place better than I."

"Just get some sleep; everything is in good hands. Half the day is gone, and I need to get to the office. I have a deposition hearing in the morning. If you need something, I'll make other arrangements."

Ben leaned onto his pillow with his arms crossed on his chest. "Don't worry about it, I'm fine. This is just an inconvenience; a painful one, but just an inconvenience."

****

Ben hated hospitals. He did not feel like a patient; he felt like a prisoner. The only thing keeping him there was his inability to get up, which had as much to do with pain medicine as the surgical procedure itself. It made him sleep, but when he awoke in unfamiliar surroundings it momentarily frightened him. By late evening he made progress and was able to stand, but he was attached to an IV pole. The nurses told him not to get out of bed without assistance. He wanted his own clothes and was determined to get home as soon as possible. The only person he trusted to help him was Nora. He grimaced and clutched his side as he reached for the phone. As he listened for the ring, he tapped his fingers on his bedstand waiting for her to answer. When she did, he exhaled the breath he was holding. "Nora?"

"Yes, Mr. Stafford. How are you feeling?"

"I have been better, but I want to come home as soon as possible. Please put together a change of clothing and bring them to the hospital tomorrow morning?"

"Are they discharging you so soon?"

There was silence, then he replied, "Probably not, but as soon as I can get out the door I will. I just want sweats, something loose fitting and easy to pull on. Barring that, at least bring my robe."

****

Nora did not know what to make of his request; was he determined to come home or was he under the influence of medication? She decided it did not matter; she did as he asked. The next morning, she placed the requested items in an overnight bag and headed for the hospital. She was earlier than normal visiting hours, but she did not expect anyone to give her a difficult time about dropping off clothing. She arrived in time to overhear his physician on morning rounds tell him he was not well enough to leave.

"I can't take another day here," Ben pleaded. "You know why I hate this hospital. Just let me go home."

"I do know, but you are not ready. You still have dressings to be changed and drains to be attended; it is not advisable. Stay a little longer."

Recognizing the desperation in Ben's voice, Nora intervened. "I can do it."

She instantly regretted the offer and was not certain why she even made it. The doctor and Ben stared at her in stunned silence. "I have some experience at changing dressing and attending to drains provided there are no complications."

"See," Ben said as he pointed to Nora. "I have an expert to help me. Just *let me out!*"

"This is against my better judgement, but I will discharge you," the doctor said on a deep sigh. "At least stay through the afternoon so we can monitor your progress. In the absence of anything unforeseen, you may go home this evening."

Nora was apprehensive about her decision to care for Ben, but he gave her such a plaintive look she didn't change her mind. A nurse entered with a list of supplies she needed to get from the drug store. This was all the excuse Nora needed to leave. "I'll go track down these things; call me when you can be released."

Ben smiled and she thought he looked triumphant. He had never displayed a combative or belligerent side of his personality. She instinctively felt there was a story behind it.

The doctor honored his promise to Ben to release him if he improved throughout the day. The floor nurse called Nora and she wasted no time returning to the hospital. She found him sitting in a wheelchair, holding a bag of his clothes, and restlessly tapping his foot on its chair rest. At first sight of her, he pressed the nurses call button and one appeared. Nora bent her head to disguise a smile. The nurse seemed as anxious to discharge him as he was to leave.

An orderly transported him to the patient pick-up area, helping him into Nora's car. As she drove, she kept her eyes straight ahead on the road, saying nothing. The silence between them was awkward. He had not spoken a word since leaving the hospital parking lot, eventually he broke his silence. "I know this is not part of your job description, but I really do appreciate it."

"It's not like I have somewhere else to be. You don't strike me as the type who would linger in order to be catered to, and even if you were, that is what you pay me for."

"Ouch!" he mumbled. "I know you've been going to the Veteran's Hospital; I hope this won't interfere."

"Our agreement was I may volunteer a couple of days a week if it did not conflict with my job. This is my job and right now you need me more than they do. There is no structure to my volunteering, I come and go as I please, so don't worry about it."

Her words sounded cool, but her demeanor was soft. She was worried about his welfare but needed to keep their carefully constructed detachment. She pulled directly into the garage. He winced as he swung his legs out of the car. He clung to it like a spider on a web as he walked around to go into the house. Nora quickly grabbed one arm while he leaned on her. It seemed like her living quarters were a mile away as she struggled to help him through the kitchen. He held onto the footboard as she pulled back the covers of her bed. He dropped on it like a thrown rock, then she tucked him in as if he were a child.

"I left the light on in the bathroom, but it's a good idea to keep your phone with you if you get up. I'll have my cell phone on in my room upstairs so you can call if you need me."

"This is not how I imagined my week going. My mother always said that man makes plans and God laughs. He must find this hysterical. I will be fine, don't worry about me."

She stood in the doorway of the bedroom with a grin on her face. "Do as I suggest; in your condition I'm pretty sure I can take you."

When she was walking through the kitchen, she heard him laugh and then yell, "ouch," and laughed again.

Chapter Seven

Ben slept poorly. Part of his macho recovery was to avoid taking any painkillers, but during the night he gave in. In the hospital they nearly knocked him out but did not seem to have the same effect on him at home. At five thirty in the morning, he heard Nora in the kitchen; he put on his robe and went to see her. He was a disheveled mess, but he did not care, he wanted a cup of the coffee she was brewing. When she saw him stumbling through the kitchen hanging onto the countertop for support, she promptly pulled out a chair for him to sit.

Pointing, he said, "Coffee."

She laughed at his one-word demand. "Tea is probably a better choice."

"Probably," he acknowledged, "but I want coffee."

"Are you hungry?"

"Not really."

She picked up a pill container on the counter. "These antibiotics will stay down easier if you have food to coat your stomach. Let me at least scramble you a couple of eggs. Afterward I am going to change your dressings and check the drain tube." She reached for the eggs in the refrigerator.

"I'm too tired to argue."

"It doesn't matter if you do; I'm still going to do it. I promised the doctor."

He lifted his coffee mug to his lips and said, "It has been a long time since I've had someone take care of me. It's both nice and disconcerting."

She cracked the eggs into a measuring cup and began to beat them with a fork. "I can identify with that. I am very independent, and I don't accept help from others easily. It's not about feeling beholden, it's about being afraid of losing my edge. Sometimes we need help and should take it, if for no other reason than it's a kindness to the one who offers it."

He was stunned because it felt like she could read his mind. Ben never analyzed himself before, but Nora conveyed it better. He had conditioned himself to avoid feeling close to anyone because when they are gone it hurt too much. Both were slowly coming to the realization they were of similar mind, philosophy, and cowardice in their approach to living their lives.

After a sip of coffee, he realized she was right about the wisdom of drinking tea. The eggs went down surprisingly well but going back to bed sounded appealing. "I think I'll go lie down."

"I'll clean up here and change your dressings."

A few minutes later she came into his room with a kit filled with gloves, bandages, cotton swabs, and a topical ointment prescribed by the doctor. Ben was horrified when he noticed his pajama pants were soaked with blood. "What's that? Are my sutures open?"

Her voice was reassuring. "Relax, it's just some drainage. It's mixed with a little blood, but it's completely normal. You can expect that for a few days." After putting on the gloves, she skillfully removed the old bandages, cleared the drains, cleansed the incision area, then applied clean bandages.

"Do you think you will be able to change into some clean pajama bottoms by yourself?" she asked as she gathered up the medical supplies.

He certainly was not about to let her help him. "If I can't, Brian is stopping by on his way to work. He can help me."

Almost on cue, Brian bounced through the kitchen door and yelled, "Where is the lazy slacker? He should be at his office by now."

Nora handed him a muffin with a strong cup of coffee. "Don't encourage him or he's apt to go."

Ben heard his friend and called out, "Get your sorry butt in here; I need help."

Brian scrutinized him. "You sure look better than you did yesterday."

"Roadkill would look better than I did."

Brian bit into the muffin squirting butter down his chin. "It appears you are in capable hands."

"I think she may have been a drill sergeant in another lifetime." There was no condemnation in his voice, just sheer appreciation.

"In any event, I feel better knowing you're not alone or with some fly-by-night nurse's aid," Brian replied.

Ben propped himself up on his pillows. "Believe me, I am too. I hate to ask you, but can you help me change into clean pajamas?"

Brian grabbed a fresh pair and was careful not to disturb the incision and drain. "Just like our old college days when you were too drunk to do this for yourself."

Ben's eyes widened and his voice squeaked, "That was you, not me."

"Oh, yes, I guess it was. This must be payback."

Ben shook his head. "How you ever got through college and law school, I'll never know." He admired Brian's zest for life and deep down understood his friend was serious minded when it came to his career.

For the next couple of days, Ben let himself be Nora's patient which was a far superior alternative to the hospital. He was walking around more and even sat on the terrace. Autumn was in the air and sometimes it was too cool to stay outside for extended periods. Nora encouraged him to stay on the patio as much as possible. The fresh air and pleasure of his garden were better medicine than anything the doctor may have prescribed. The cooler evenings were mitigated by the fall beauty of his gardens. It was sacrilege for him not to enjoy his long vigorous efforts in tending the garden. Nora placed a hand stitched quilt around him and pushed him out the door to enjoy a hot cup of cocoa and the crisp air. As he gratefully sipped the sweet, smooth liquid, he realized it was just what he needed to recover. By the week's end he returned to the doctor; he no longer needed a drain, and his incision was healing. He was sleeping in his own bedroom and started going to the office on a part-time trial. He decided to tell Nora to move her things back to her room when he found her in the kitchen on a small ladder adjusting a curtain. He called out to her.

"Just a minute. This darn thing has been driving me crazy."

He stopped midsentence when he saw her reaching above her head with her arms in the air. It caused her shirt to ride up exposing her stomach. She had an exceptionally long scar which traveled down her entire mid-section to beneath the waistband of her pants. Its irregularity made it impossible for it to be the result of any surgery. It was raised and purple, proving it was not years old. No wonder she knew what to do for him, she must have gone through something devastating to cause such a scar. Fortunately, she did not notice what he was staring at, and he wasn't about to inquire. That violated their tacit code.

The phone rang and Ben said, "I'll get it."

He wished he had let the answering machine pick it up. It was his mother, and she was less than pleased she had to find out about his surgery from a secretary in his office. She called his office because he had not answered any of her messages. It was completely out of character for him. He was waiting to feel better before he spoke with her.

"I'm sorry, Mom. I knew you'd worry, so I was waiting. Yes, I'm fine. I will be returning to work full time next week." He waited for her to respond then said, "Yes, I guess so. Not a problem, I will be looking forward to it. Bye." He put the phone back on the receiver and stood staring at it like it was going to bite him.

"Something wrong?" Nora asked as she stepped down from the ladder.

"Define wrong. My mother is coming in two weeks. She will be bringing my sister and niece. I have never met my niece because she was born in Sweden. My brother-in-law was transferred there but now they are returning to the States. My sister came first and is staying with my mother until her husband can join them. They thought it an excellent opportunity for me to see them and reassure my mother I'm not dying."

Nora folded the ladder and was carrying it to the

pantry. "You don't want them to come?"

"I wouldn't say that. I love them both and it's been years since I've seen my sister."

"But," Nora finished for him. "You're not happy about having your routine interrupted."

"Exactly; not to mention its more work for you. You can hire extra help if you need; just call the agency."

"That's not necessary. I worked at an inn, remember? This won't be much different. Three more people are nothing. The guest rooms are ready so I will just buy food a child may like. They can be finnicky."

"I'll ask my mother if there should be any special arrangements, but I doubt it. My sister runs a pretty tight ship."

Nora pulled out a chair for him to sit and slid a bowl of fruit toward him. He peeled a banana as he listened to her. "I know about keeping children content. We had a steady stream of them through the inn. If you don't have any toys or games, I can pick up a few along with some coloring books."

His cheeks puffed as he blew out an air of relief. "Yes, anything she might like. I cannot begin to know what kids need to keep happy."

"It's almost Halloween and if your niece hasn't been in the United States, she probably hasn't experienced one. Do you want me to decorate the house?"

He had not decorated for the holidays in years. It was not that he did not enjoy seeing them in other people's homes, but it seemed like a ridiculous amount of work when he lived alone. He had neither the patience nor ambition to decorate and then put them all away after the holiday passed. "That's too much to ask of you on top of the extra work with my family."

It was the first time he had seen Nora excited. "I welcome the diversion. Every holiday was acknowledged at the inn; the patrons expected it. I looked forward to it."

He shrugged. "If you want to, far be it from me to discourage it. I don't want to over burden you, you're already going the extra mile."

"Do you have any decorations?"

He rubbed his forehead. "That was never my department, but there is a sundry of boxes in the basement. If you don't find anything, buy what you want. They have all kinds of new things since I last decorated. Halloween has become as popular as Christmas when it comes to decorations."

"I will keep it to the fun things like carved pumpkins, witches smashed into trees and such. I don't want to frighten her with ghouls and skeletons."

Ben smiled and made a saluting gesture. "Those details never even occur to me. I really appreciate that they do to you. I believe I'm putting my home in the hands of a trained expert."

"It was my job, I tried to match the decorations with the people. After running the inn for a couple of years, I noticed patterns of age, whether they were likely to bring children, be single or married. It is kind of nice to know what I've learned hasn't gone to waste."

Ben leaned in and asked, "Do all those things really matter?"

She shrugged. "I guess it would depend on what you consider *matters*. Our level of service never varied, but it's the little things which remain in people's hearts. It often was the difference between repeat business or them choosing someplace else to stay when they return to the area."

Ben traveled frequently on business matters, so when searching his recollections, he realized she was right. There were places he sometimes went out of his way to stay for just that reason.

****

Nora was in her element. All the things she enjoyed about the inn she applied to her new job. Decorating lightened her spirits and for the first time she was certain her decision to leave her home was the right one. She was balancing the best of the old with the new. Despite Ben's reluctance about having his family visit, Nora thought it was good for him. If he was half as frightened about his emergency surgery as she was, it seemed important to have his family close. Were it not for Brian, she didn't know who to contact when Ben's appendix ruptured. She never applied that same possibility to herself.

Autumn was her favorite time of year. Ben's garden and yard were a joy to walk through. The trees were in varying degrees of green, gold, and crimson. The roses were still blooming and continued to hang onto their buds until the frost. Many of the perennials and annuals were waning, however the chrysanthemums were spectacular in their peak. Ben had surgically removed the dead and dying plants. Nora took advantage of his enormous yard and sectioned it off into areas with varying Halloween themes. She had silly inflatable ghosts and black cats, pumpkins and non-scary witches scattered throughout the yard.

Orange and gold twinkling lights dangled from the tree branches. She reserved her resources for the backyard, keeping in mind it was intended to enchant a child. On the front of the house, she hung a simple fall wreath on the door, scattered a dozen pumpkins around amidst corn stalks and colorful Indian corn. She noticed neighbors walking by to examine her work leading her to conclude it was something new to them. One person even gave her a discreet thumbs-up sign.

No one enjoyed her efforts more than Brian. He was like a kid in a candy shop. He came over one afternoon while she was strategically placing the ornaments and lights and insisted upon coming back at night for what he called a "trial run." Three acres never seemed so large as he ran around the yard darting in and out of the maze of decorations. He even brought a ghost costume. As he ran around booing and hooing, Ben and Nora just watched in awe. Nora finally spoke up in an amused tone, "He is your best friend? Why?"

Ben's eyes followed Brian during his mad tear through the yard. "I'm not entirely certain."

Brian was panting for breath as he plopped into a chair. "This is great. Why haven't you done this before?"

Ben snorted. "Because unlike you, I'm sane."

Brian playfully slapped Ben's leg. "We all need a little insanity when it's this much fun."

Nora just shook her head and went inside to make them an Irish coffee. When she handed it to them, it was Ben, this time, who said, "Please; join us."

She uncharacteristically let down her defenses and joined them. She sat with them looking out upon her creation. It was fun and whimsical, and she was proud of herself. At the inn she bargain shopped and repurposed things to decorate. Ben gave her free rein to do what she wanted, and it showed. It was a pleasure to work with an unlimited budget, however her thrifty nature kept her in check. For this one night she agreed they were not employer/employee, they were three friends enjoying the experience. Brian seemed to appreciate the simple, good clean fun. He clinked his cup against Ben and Nora's. "To Nora and her ability to turn a backyard into a land of enchantment."

"To Nora," Ben repeated lifting his cup. "I can't remember the last time I celebrated Halloween."

Brian had just taken a big sip from his mug and started laughing so hard the Irish coffee shot out of his nose. "That's because you're too stuffy to enjoy it. You were the only holdout not wearing a costume at the country club masquerade party."

Ben's head shot up and his voice had a light clip to it. "That's because you make enough fool of yourself for both of us."

Brian wiped his nose on the back of his sleeve. "I resemble that remark."

Nora interrupted their banter. "To Mr. Stafford's niece."

They all said, "Here, here." Despite the light-heartedness of the moment, Nora thought she caught a glimpse of sadness on Ben's face.

"Making a child's life fun and carefree is the greatest gift anyone can give. I remember once when I lost a tooth, and I placed it under my pillow for the tooth fairy. My grandfather had a snoot full and instead of placing a dollar it was a hundred-dollar bill. I tried to pull a couple of others out," Brian quipped.

Ben replied, "At least I know where you got your penchant for drinking. If you keep it up, you'll lose a few more."

With a haughty lift of his head, Brian said, "Hey, I have a partial plate because of an accident."

Ben had a smirk on his face. "The *accident* was a fall down the Country Club stairs when you were dead drunk."

"An accident is an accident," Brian replied flipping his hand in the air.

Nora shook her head as she watched the exchange between these old friends. "And with that I will retire for the evening. Good night, gentlemen."

****

Brian watched as Nora disappeared into the house. "I want to be you."

Ben never looked up; he drained the rest of his coffee. "Nobody should ever want to be me; certainly not you. I'd give you some of *my* teeth if I to have your life."

In a muted voice Brian said, "It isn't all it seems either, my old friend."

Ben got to his feet. "Let's go get a real drink."

Chapter Eight

The big day finally arrived when Ben's family flew into the local airport. Nora meticulously covered all bases by predicting any of their needs. She was not used to anyone being in the house except Ben. For all the months she worked for him, there were never any guests accept Brian McNair. She was accustomed to inn guests coming and going, but she enjoyed the solitude of the empty house. She needed to please only one person and not a dozen guests at a time, nevertheless she found herself looking forward to serving them.

Nora and Ben continued to keep their structured formality as always, but his recent illness softened their boundaries. Casual conversation when passing through the house was now frequent, however, with the arrival of his mother, sister, and niece she decided to convey a strict employer/employee relationship.

At noon, the phone rang. "Nora," Ben said on the call from his office. "I'm really, reeeally sorry, but I need you to pick my family up at the airport. Normally I'd never ask this of you. There are some complications in this meeting I am in, and I just can't leave yet. I promise I will be home as soon as feasibly possible."

Taken off guard, she stuttered when she replied, "Ah, I, I guess so."

There was genuine gratitude and relief in the sound of his voice. "Thank you. Take my SUV because I am not sure how much stuff they brought with them. I will text my sister to let her know what happened and to expect you."

The airport was only thirty minutes away and an easy drive. As airports go, it was on a smaller scale and not as congested as those in larger cities. It still offered direct flights to all the major cities. She parked as close to the entrance as possible because she knew Mrs. Stafford was in ill health. Ben gave her the flight number and arrival time; she went inside and waited at the gate. They were among the first to disembark the plane. Nora recognized them by Ben's description. Mrs. Stafford was an attractive but frail woman with silver hair coiffed to perfection. Ben's sister looked very much like him in female form, and his niece was an adorable little girl with large blue eyes and long auburn pigtails. Nora stepped forward. "Mrs. Stafford?"

The three stopped and she said, "You must be Nora."

"Yes."

Mrs. Stafford pointed to her daughter. "This is Benjamin's sister, Libby Frazier and my granddaughter Sarah."

There was such pride in her voice when she introduced Sarah it made Nora smile. The little girl clutched her doll and uttered a meek, "Hi."

"I'll help you with your bags," Nora said as they headed for the baggage claim. There was more luggage than she had expected. "I'll bring the car curbside; it will be easier for you."

She pulled the SUV up to the door, then jumped out to help the family. Libby assisted her mother into the front seat and buckled Sarah in the car seat, while

Nora placed their bags in the back. She tried to remain as impersonal as possible, but they insisted upon asking her questions and involving her in their conversation. During their drive Mrs. Stafford asked, "How is my son, really? I was so angry he didn't call about his operation."

Nora spoke in a calm voice to downplay his ordeal. "He is doing very well. Appendectomies are routine these days. He won't be playing handball or golf for a while but other than that he's healing nicely."

"I am relieved you were in the house to take him to the hospital and then care for him during his recovery." Mrs. Stafford was flexing her fist as she spoke, which did not go unnoticed by Nora.

Libby steered the subject away from Ben's health. "I'm anxious for him to meet Sarah. She was born while we were in Sweden; they have never met. Mother came over a few times, but Ben never made it. It's a shame, because it is such a beautiful country."

"It is a long journey. I didn't visit as often as I would have liked. I only made the trip during Sweden's summer season," Mrs. Stafford said.

"I can appreciate your reluctance. I understand the weather can be bitter cold," Nora replied.

Usually children chatter up a storm, but Sarah sat quietly playing with her doll and singing something in Swedish.

"Is she fluent in Swedish?" Nora asked to keep the conversation impersonal.

"Yes, she is now, but I doubt she will remember it when she gets older. It's not a language used much in the US," Libby answered.

Nora's face softened as she smiled. "She's a very

well-behaved little girl, especially considering the long journey she recently made."

Libby snorted. "She is a sweetheart right now but she's exhausted and needs a nap. Once she is recharged, we can't keep up with her."

Nora turned into the quiet cul-du-sac and Libby commented, "It's even more beautiful than I remember. Look, Sarah, there are cornstalks and scarecrows." The little girl's head popped up and looked out the window as she giggled.

"Mr. Stafford decorated for Halloween assuming Sarah had not experienced one," Nora said giving him all the credit.

"That was very sweet of him to think of that," Libby replied.

Mrs. Stafford was silent as she admired the decorations. "He hasn't decorated since…." She did not finish her sentence.

Nora pulled the car up to the front entrance to help Mrs. Stafford and unload the car. She unlocked the front door and ushered them into the foyer. "I will bring your bags up for you. Mrs. Stafford, I've prepared the first room on the right for you, and, Mrs. Frazier, yours is the second on the left. Mr. Stafford said you wanted Sarah in the room with you."

"Yes, we've traveled so much she is getting a little anxious without me, so I think it is best."

"That's quite common. I used to work in an inn and most of the parents preferred to keep their children in the same room because of the unfamiliar surroundings."

The family went upstairs to their rooms to unpack and rest. Nora tried to think of anything which might add to their comfort, especially in Libby's room. She arranged fresh fruit and a small dish of chocolate candies for Sarah. When she carried their suitcases to their rooms, they expressed their genuine appreciation. Nora treated them like guests at the inn by predicting their needs. "I'll have refreshments for you in the living room whenever it is convenient for you."

Libby looked at her mother. "Mom needs to rest for a while, and I know Sarah is ready for a nap. We will wait for my brother."

Nora spoke in her most professional voice, "Whenever you're ready, please let me know."

****

An hour later, after returning home, Ben looked around the house but did not see his family anywhere. He sought Nora who was in her usual place, the kitchen. She looked up from her prep work when he said, "I'm really sorry I did this to you. I didn't have much choice unless I told them to take a taxi. I didn't want to do that."

"It wasn't a problem, really. They are genuinely nice people, and your niece is a real doll."

"Where are they?"

"Resting." No sooner had Nora spoken when Libby came running through the house and hugged Ben so hard, he had to push her away. "Oh, Benji, I'm sorry I forgot about your operation. It's just so good to see you. You've gotten gray," she said in a mocking tone.

"And you've put on weight."

She giggled. "Ouch, I'll never learn."

"Where's Mom?"

"She and Sarah are napping. I am so glad we are finally back in the US; I didn't like being far away from Mom."

Ben turned to Nora but before he asked, she handed him a bourbon and a glass of white wine. He smiled and nodded his appreciation. "We'll be in the music room."

****

He chose the music room, which was rarely used, because the piano once belonged to their grandmother. It was special to them. It was a shameful embarrassment neither of them played better than at an elementary level, but it was a beautiful instrument. Libby walked up to it, opened the cover on the keys, and ran her fingers across it. "It's in tune!"

"You can thank Nora. She told me leaving it out of tune for too long is bad for it. It then requires more tuning than normal."

"Where'd you find her, by the way?" she asked.

He sighed. "She is the last, I hope, of a long line of housekeeper/cooks the employment agency sent me. I guess if you try long enough, you're bound to find the right one."

"She seems very efficient, but awfully quiet. We had to drag conversation out of her."

"That's just her nature. I'm much the same. It is one of the many things I appreciate about her."

"Benjamin, is that you?" He heard his mother call from the top of the stairs.

He bolted up the stairs and gave her a bear hug and kiss. "It's so good to see you, Mom."

She playfully slapped him. "I'm still mad at you."

"I know, Mom, I'm a bad boy," he said kissing her again.

His family was particularly important to him even if they did not live in the same state. He held her arm and safely escorted her to the bottom of the stairs and into the music room. Nora promptly appeared. "May I get something for you, Mrs. Stafford?"

She looked from her daughter to her son, paused for a moment, and with a guilty giggle she responded, "I'll have what he's having."

"Mom!" Libby said aghast. "It'll knock you on your butt."

"Libby, I'm old and I'm tired, but still your mother. Nora, bring me the drink."

Nora looked at her boss who shrugged. She smiled as she replied, "Immediately, Mrs. Stafford."

A couple of minutes later Nora appeared with the drink on a tray and an array of hors d'oeuvres. Mrs. Stafford took a long sip, bent her head backward, and sighed. "I love that woman."

Ben had forgotten how good it felt to be in the presence of his family; they were fun, kind, and compassionate. They spent the next hour catching up on the last five years. "When is Jason coming home?" Ben asked of his sister's husband.

Libby had stuffed her mouth with appetizers and held her finger up to halt her answer until she could swallow. "In a couple of weeks; he has a few loose ends to tidy up and then he will join us at Mom's."

"Where will you be living?"

"The company gave him a choice of San Francisco, Chicago, or Charleston. We chose Charleston."

"That's great, you'll be near Mom."

"Not just Mom, Jason's parents are only forty-five minutes from there. It will give Sarah the opportunity to know her grandparents."

Ben turned to his mother. "This must thrill you."

Mrs. Stafford reached over to squeeze Libby's hand. "It does. I'm still independent, but it gives me a sense of security to know family is close by."

Ben bent over to kiss her cheek. "You know you are always welcome to live here."

"Oh, Ben, that was not a condemnation. I know I am welcome in both your homes if the need arises. It's just too darn cold here."

Ben was about to say something when they heard a frantic, "Mommy, Mommy."

Libby jumped to her feet. "The princess is awake. I'll be right back."

Libby returned carrying Sarah down the stairs and into the music room. She ushered her daughter over to her brother. "Sarah, this is Mommy's brother; your Uncle Ben."

She clung to her mother's leg uncertain of a new person. Libby said in a reassuring voice, "It's okay, he won't bite."

Ben felt lightheaded and a sweaty surge ran through his body as he stared at the child. He stammered when he said, "Hello, Sarah. It's very nice to meet you." He extended his hand, so she was not forced to hug or kiss a complete stranger.

The child ventured forward and shook his hand. "You have a pretty house," she said.

"Thank you. We have some surprises for you while you're here."

As excited as children are when a surprise is dangled before them, she asked, "What? Where are they?"

Libby stroked Sarah's hair. "Don't be rude, Sarah, Uncle Ben will show you in due time."

Nora appeared with a glass of chocolate milk and a plate of cookies. Sarah ran right up to her to devour the treats.

"Not too many, I'm sure Nora has a nice dinner cooking for you," her grandmother cautioned.

"I'll just eat these," the child replied, and everyone laughed except Ben who had grown quiet.

Nora returned to her duties leaving the family alone, but Ben excused himself and abruptly left the room. He stood in the hallway taking deep breaths and absently stared out the front door. Libby followed him. "Are you feeling all right? You can go lie down if you need to; don't feel as though you have to entertain us."

He swallowed hard, took a deep breath, and spewed, "You could have warned me." He stormed off to the sunroom. He felt himself begin to shake. Nora was in the pantry, so he thought he was alone. He took his wallet from his pocket and opened it to stare at a photograph tucked in its fold.

Nora walked past him balancing fruits and vegetables in preparation for dinner when she casually looked over his shoulder. "What a cute picture of Sarah."

He was so absorbed in his thoughts he was startled when she spoke. He shoved the picture back in his wallet and said with a growl. "That's not Sarah." He sprinted off and went upstairs to his bedroom.

****

A pall fell over the music room but gratefully it was short lived when Brian bounded through the front door and gleefully shouted, "Where are my best girls?" Libby ran to him with the same enthusiasm she had for Ben. He picked her up and spun her around in a circle, planting a big kiss on her lips.

"I've missed you," she said laughing.

Cocking his head to one side and speaking in a mischievous voice, "Anna, you're going to get a big kiss, too."

Mrs. Stafford giggled. "Don't you ever grow up?"

"There's never been any fun in it."

He spotted Sarah across the room. "And who do we have here?"

Libby took her hand and led her up to Brian. He suppressed a gasp when she approached him, but he quickly recovered.

"Sarah, this is Brian, your Uncle Ben's closest friend."

Unlike Ben, he wasn't reserved with the child. "You can call me Uncle Brian if you like." He swept her up into the air, spinning her around just as he did with her mother to the same excited screams. His eyes scanned the room. "Where is the lord of the manor?"

Anna said, "I believe he is in his bedroom."

Brian sprang up the stairs and without bothering to knock he barged into Ben's room. Ben was lying on the bed staring at the ceiling. "Get out," he said in a soft but adamant tone.

Brian plopped down on the bed beside him. "No."

Ben's eyes remained transfixed on the ceiling. "You saw her?"

He nodded. "It's not the kid's fault."

"Maybe not."

Brian's tenor was severe. "There is no maybe about it. Look, there is no one I am closer to and care more about than you. I say this with love; get your sorry butt downstairs and give Sarah the Halloween you and Nora planned for her."

Ben did not have the opportunity to respond when they heard a gentle knock and the door opened. It was Libby. Ben sat up on the edge of the bed as she ran over to him and threw her arms around him. "I'm so sorry. I love you and I would never do anything to hurt you. We will leave in the morning."

Ben's head dropped and a tear trickled down his cheek. "No, please don't. Brian was right and I am being selfishly ridiculous. Let me pull myself together and I will be down." He looked at Brian. "You can leave now and go down with Libby."

Brian threw his hands in the air. "The only thing I heard is Brian is right; music to my ears."

The corner of Ben's mouth turned up. "Do you ever stop being a jerk?"

He slapped Ben on the back and gave Libby a little kiss on the cheek. "I'm the comic relief, my friend."

Brian's levity got him in as much trouble as often as it helped, but there was never any question among all who knew him that his heart was always in the right place.

Chapter Nine

Ben reluctantly joined his family in the music room; he apologized to everyone but directed his comments to Sarah. "I'm very sorry that I haven't seemed like I was in a good mood. I'm still getting well after my operation. I hope you can forgive me, and I promise to do better. After dinner we will give you your surprise."

Nora peeked into the room and asked Ben, "Sir, do you wish for me to serve dinner or arrange it family style?"

He looked around the room at everyone when his sister replied, "Definitely family style, Nora. I don't want you to have to deal with Sarah's picky selections."

"I expected that and made child friendly foods. Will Mr. McNair be joining you?"

"Of course, you don't think I'd miss one of your meals," Brian said. He looked at the women gathered. "Wait until you girls eat one of Nora's creations. You will never want to go home."

She brought in platters and bowls of food, setting them in easy reach for Ben to pass. She then disappeared back into the kitchen. Sarah gulped her food down. It was clear she hoped to rush everyone to get to her surprise.

"Slow down," her mother admonished.

Jumping up and down on her chair she said, "I

can't, I want to see what Uncle Ben has for me."

The adults decided to be accommodating and put off dessert until later. "You'll need your coat, it's cold outside," Ben cautioned.

Everyone bundled up and went out onto the dark patio. Nora stayed behind. She had set up the decorations, but Ben wired them to a remote control, so they turned on simultaneously to maximize the effect. He handed Sarah the remote and said, "Okay, now push the button."

Her tiny fingers pushed down on the button with all their might. The entire yard lit up to the delight of not just Sarah but her mother and grandmother. Brian whispered to Ben, "It's like I'm seeing it again for the first time. Just look at the delight on Sarah's face."

"Oh, Ben," Libby said. "How fun, it must have taken you days to do this. I have never seen anything like it."

"I'd like to take the credit, but Nora is responsible. I just connected the cords to the remote control."

"Well, whoever is responsible, you have just made a little girl extremely happy. She is absolutely mesmerized," Anna said.

In an instant Sarah was off running through the yard but her excitement, as great as it was, paled next to Brian's during the sneak preview. The trees and bushes had pumpkin and ghost string lights wrapped around them and witches dangling from the trees. Brian ran ahead of her to make sure she saw all there was to see and find the pumpkin basket filled with candy.

Sarah's mother and grandmother watched with amusement. The cool night air was filled with screams of delight and laughter as Brian took Sarah on the adventure. Ben wasn't laughing like everyone else. He sat stone faced, letting only his eyes follow Sarah's mad dash through the maze of decorations. He discreetly slipped away into the kitchen where Nora was preparing dessert. "You should be out there, you did all the work," Ben told her.

"This is a family moment; I don't want to be in the way," she said as she rinsed dishes in the sink.

He looked out the window with a somber expression on his face. "Neither do I."

At that instance Brian went screaming by with Sarah hot on his trail and then they disappeared into the shrubs. Nora smiled. "He's really just a big kid, isn't he?"

Ben's eyes followed the duo until they vanished in the yard. "I'm a little jealous of his carefree, fun-loving manner. Everyone adores him, even my family. I wish I were more like him."

Glancing out the window again, Nora replied, "Sometimes we envy people out of ignorance."

There was more kindness in her words than she knew, but Ben did. Brian seemed so content in his carefree lifestyle, but Ben was aware there was little substance to it. He also knew with substance came potential pain.

The next couple of days were uneventful, which was a blessing for everyone. Mrs. Stafford was satisfied her son was well and in the capable hands of Nora. Libby and Ben were closer than ever, but everyone was ready to say goodbye. The Stafford family left with hugs and kisses for everyone, even Nora. Before leaving, Mrs. Stafford privately pulled Nora aside. "I know we do not know each other, but I instantly sensed you were a kind and caring person. It is a great relief for me to know you are here to take care of him."

She patted her hands. "That's very kind of you to say, Mrs. Stafford, but I don't think he needs anyone to care for him." With a laugh she added, "Provided he doesn't have two appendices."

"He needs someone more than you are aware," Mrs. Stafford replied and then pinched Nora's cheek. "Thank you, child."

Ben dropped them off at the airport. Upon his return, he said, "I appreciate your help, Nora. You went above and beyond for my family. I'm not afraid to say I survived only with your help."

"That's very nice of you, but I don't think that's true. I never met nicer people in my life, and they exemplify unconditional love."

"They do, and I know how lucky I am to have them." He asked, "Is it awful I'm glad they're gone?"

Nora chuckled. "No, tacky perhaps, but not awful. Family are the people who know us best, and sometimes we don't want to be reminded of that."

"I think Brian will miss them more than I will. He told me has a new girlfriend, so I'll probably be seeing less of him."

"He will always have time for you. I cannot imagine any woman coming between you."

It was Ben's turn to laugh. "She won't last long enough for me to find out. He goes through girlfriends like I go through paperclips. I don't think he wants to be in a relationship."

****

Nora returned to her volunteer work at the Veterans' Hospital. Between Ben's operation and his family coming into town, she had been absent for three weeks. Veterans Day was approaching, and from past experience she knew the hospitals went to great lengths to celebrate. The patients typically rally around one another, but Veterans Day was extra special. The average citizen too, takes the time to honor them. A party in the main dining hall was planned and the volunteers were encouraged to contribute by making refreshments. Nora contributed by paying for all the ingredients she needed to do the baking. She felt obliged to ask Mr. Stafford's permission to use the kitchen. She doubted he would object, but she did not want to take liberties without his consent. He was more than accommodating and even offered to pay for the supplies she needed, but she refused to accept. It was her donation and did not feel it was proper to accept money from him. It was enough for her to use his kitchen.

"It's kind of you to offer financial help but it isn't necessary. I need the day off if you don't mind. I do not know how long I'll be there, and my boyfriend may have plans."

"Boyfriend?" he echoed at a higher pitch than normal.

"Yep," she replied with humor in her voice. "He said the only thing that kept him going in Anzio was knowing he was coming home to me."

Ben smiled at the World War II reference. "How old is he, ninety?"

"Ninety-six, but he thinks he's twenty-five."

"If you're going to have a delusion, being young with a pretty woman is a good place to start." She blushed at being called pretty. It was the most personal thing he ever said to her.

"Don't worry about anything, just have fun. My office will be closed, so I think I will spend the day cutting out the rest of the dying flowers in the garden. There is nothing so depressing as looking at dead blooms; as it is, I miss the Halloween decorations."

"There's always Thanksgiving."

He looked out the window with a sad expression. "By then there won't be a hint of anything left."

****

Nora baked red, white, and blue cupcakes sprinkled with silver glittered sugar and added a tiny flag to each one. Her biggest concern was transporting them without crushing the frosting. She never drove so carefully in her entire life while moving them to their destination. They were a tremendous success, and her *boyfriend* ate three of them. The local high school band and chorus students gave up their holiday to entertain the disabled soldiers. They even stayed to help with the cleanup.

Nora walked among the veterans who were mobile enough to gather in the recreation area. The fortunate ones were attended by family members, but sadly there were some with no one by their side. Nora's special friend Vincent was among them, but he was always good natured and seldom sad. There were days when he was confused, believing he lived in another era. The days when he was perfectly lucid, Nora found his kindness and wisdom to be inspirational. He playfully amused her by sometimes baiting her when he pretended he did not know he was living in the present. It did not take her long to realize when he was serious and when he was confused. It didn't matter, because in either state of mind he was a perfect gentleman. Today was a good day for him; he pointed to one of the residents. "Go sit with," and then gave her the name. He had good instincts in knowing who needed a little cheering up.

Nora was glad she was taking the time to take part in the celebration. There were days when it was emotionally challenging for her to volunteer. It was worth the effort, especially with patients like Vincent.

The day flew by, and it was late afternoon before she headed for home. Despite Ben telling her to take the entire day off, she wanted to prepare dinner for him. She stocked the refrigerator with healthy choices for him to make a meal, but she wanted to serve him something hot. He told her he would be working in the garden all day and the weather had turned cold. Hot soup seemed the logical option.

As she was pulling into the driveway, she saw a car parked at the front of the house. When she entered the foyer, she saw Ben sitting in the living room having a conversation with a woman. She only saw the back of her head and wondered who was visiting on a holiday. Mr. Stafford never conducted business at home. He looked up and motioned for her to come into the room. The woman jumped to her feet and ran to Nora embracing her and crying to the point of hysterics.

Ben wasted little time vacating the room. After he closed the door behind him, Nora asked, "Pat, how did you find me?"

****

Ben had no idea who the woman was or why she wanted to speak with Nora. He had just come inside from the garden when the doorbell rang. He found an elderly woman standing at the door inquiring if Nora was at home. No one ever came to the house to see her. His imagination ran rampant with possibilities. The woman's demeanor allowed him to assume she was from Nora's past, not someone she met after coming under his employ. When she asked after Nora, he said, "She's volunteering at the Veterans' Hospital today for the holiday."

The woman nodded. "That sounds like something she would do. Have you any idea when she will return?"

He shook his head. "Probably soon, but she has the day off so she may have other plans."

He thought she seemed distraught as she bit her lip. "It's really important I see her. May I wait outside in my car until she returns?"

Ben was torn because he did not know who this woman was, what she wanted with Nora, or if Nora even wanted to speak with her. She was not threatening in any way, so he invited her in.

"You may wait in the living room," he told her before ushering her in. He was sitting with her when Nora came home, then respectfully left them alone.

****

After wrapping her arms around Nora's neck, Pat Bauer cried hysterically. Nora gently pulled her arms away from her neck and stepped backward to look at her. Pat was gasping for air as she wiped her running nose with her hand. Nora took her by the wrist and guided her down the hallway to her living quarters. She repeated her question, "Pat, how did you find me?"

"Don and I hired a private investigator. We have known where you were for weeks, but we hoped you'd come home on your own. He wanted to come with me, but he still isn't well."

"Is it his heart?" Nora asked.

She nodded. "Your leaving was terribly hard on him. We love you so much."

Nora bent her head. "I don't know why; I thought my leaving might spare you more heartbreak."

"How can you possibly believe that? We love you, Nora. We have always loved you; nothing and no one can ever change that. Please, please come home."

Nora turned away from Pat; it was difficult for her to even look at her. "I can't, at least not yet. I need to be anonymous for once. No one here knows anything about me, and I want to keep it that way. You didn't tell Mr. Stafford anything, did you?"

"No, I would never say anything. It's no one's business. I told him it was important I speak to you and nothing more. He was very gracious about letting me wait. He seems like a truly kind and understanding person."

"Good." Nora exhaled in relief. "This is the perfect place for me right now. It's quiet; nothing is expected of me except to cook and clean. I need this time to heal, Pat. Please understand. I am sorry about Don, but reassure him I'm okay. I didn't think my leaving would cause him so much concern."

Pat put her arms around Nora and hugged her so hard Nora again had to pull away. "Of course, he's concerned. You are deeply loved. Nothing can turn back the clock, but as much as I don't agree with your decision to leave, I can understand you need a little time. Just promise me you will keep in touch; don't ever make us worry like this again."

She hugged Pat, suppressing the tears she was

determined never to shed again, and promised to periodically call them. She had been completely selfish and thoughtless by leaving without telling them, but she was afraid they might try to stop her. Nora then ushered Pat to the door, gave her one last embrace, and she was gone. After Nora closed the door, she pressed her head against the warm wood trying not to cry.

Ben came out of his library and locked eyes with her. They stood staring at one another in silence. Finally, Nora spoke. "I'm sorry if you were disrupted by my guest. I promise you it will never happen again; I had no idea she was coming here."

There was no anger in his voice when he spoke. "I was not disrupted. She was very polite and said it was important for her to see you. I will admit I was a little surprised to have someone come to my door looking for you, but you are more than welcome to have guests."

"It was presumptuous of her to visit without calling first," Nora said in way of an explanation.

His eyes were trained on her, but she detected no suspicion on his part when he asked, "Is there something you need to tell me?"

"No. My unexpected guest in no way will affect my job performance. You can depend on it."

"I wasn't concerned. I am worried about you and why you are so clearly upset. Can I at least know who came to my home?"

"She is my mother-in-law."

"Brian mentioned to me on his first visit here while I was gone you told him you weren't divorced."

Her chin dropped to her chest. "I'm not."

Chapter Ten

Ben felt his heart sink. What did he just witness? A mother-in-law meant a husband. Where is he? He was keenly aware of several possible explanations. Unnerved, he paced the floor of his office. It did nothing to calm him, so he went to his standby panacea and poured himself a drink. The warmth of the bourbon felt familiar and comforting but it held no answers. He knew how to get those answers but was not certain he wanted them. He could make a call to the employment agency or, easier yet, the Internet. He opened his laptop, went to the search engine but stopped after typing Nora. He stared at her name, then slammed the lid shut. He wasn't entirely certain if it was because he trusted her or didn't want his predictable life to alter. The truth was somewhere in the middle.

Ben never discussed what happened with Nora or anyone else, including and especially Brian. It did nothing to change his opinion of her except to realize she was as human as he. He was ashamed of himself for not realizing it earlier. Nora was always so efficient and independent. He never questioned his good fortune in having her work for him. The fact she was as introverted as he, was a plus. She needed no effort on his part. For the first time, he realized she was not happy and hiding behind her need to be completely competent and occupied in the service of another.

****

Nora prayed Ben would not pry. She knew he could easily ferret out her worst nightmare. A simple Internet search would reveal her past. Their life together was safe and functional in their impersonal relationship. She needed to keep it that way.

Why did Pat have to find her? Nora played the consequences out in her head dozens of times. She walked on eggshells every time she crossed paths with Ben. He was indifferently polite and never asked her a single question about her mother-in-law. She knew few people who would let such a bombshell slide. If he had asked, she wasn't certain what she would tell him. She decided not to question her good fortune.

****

Thanksgiving rapidly approached. It was the first major holiday since her employment with Ben. She doubted Ben expected much from her given his solitary lifestyle. Her training from the inn brought out the desire to acknowledge, if not, celebrate it. Guests often traveled during the holidays specifically to experience a festive vacation. She never disappointed them. "Sir, do you have any plans for Thanksgiving?"

By his response, one holiday seemed much like the next. "Not really. If he is in between his wife and various girlfriends, Brian and I usually go to the country club. They have a lavish Thanksgiving menu. Since he has a new girlfriend right now, I will go alone. If you want to take a few days off, please do. I certainly can fend for myself."

She wondered if it occurred to him to invite her to join him at the club. It was a clear violation of their unspoken rule of keeping their relationship professional. If he showed up at his country club with her, the rumor mill would start up and she imagined all the questions. *"Who is that with Ben? Does he have a girlfriend? Oh, she's the new housekeeper? How convenient!"* She honestly didn't worry for herself because she wasn't acquainted with any of his friends. Her concern was for Ben. He deserved better than to be the subject of cattiness. It was best he never suggested she be his guest.

"Thank you, I just might do that," she answered.

As it turned out, Ben ended up with plans, but not for the usual reasons as he admitted his sister Libby called to inform him their mother had a minor stroke. Mrs. Stafford was fine, according to Libby, and would not require more than two days in the hospital. His sister thought it prudent for him to fly down for the holiday.

When he told Nora, she was genuinely upset. "Mrs. Stafford is such a kind person; I hate this for her. She seemed frail during her recent visit, but I attributed it to her age. She has the spirit of a woman a fraction of her age, I'm certain the same spirit will prevail."

"I am going to leave Wednesday afternoon," he said. "This is a terrible time of year to book a last-minute flight, but I'll manage. Just lock up the house and go away if you wish; there is nothing here you need to trouble yourself with. I don't want this to hinder any plans you may have made."

"I will be fine. Give Mrs. Stafford my best and I hope she recovers quickly."

Ben's smile was weak. "She won't have it any other way. I have confidence in her ability to snap back from this."

After Ben left, Nora went to the basement and started rummaging through the Christmas decorations. Once Thanksgiving Day was over, the official start of Christmas began. She decided to get a jump on it. She hauled the tote boxes marked for the holiday and put them in the music room. She laid them out to inspect their contents and decide where to place the decorations. She stretched out strings of lights checking for blown bulbs. Garlands and wreaths were in one pile, tabletop items and ornaments in another. It was a mess but an organized one. It's something she wanted to do but didn't want to inconvenience Ben. In his absence she had the leisure of taking her time. She enjoyed decorating and was a perfectionist. She hummed carols to herself as she examined each item.

On Thanksgiving morning, she started by running a garland with lights and pinecones down the long staircase. She tied it securely to the railing with vibrant red ribbon. It instantly brought warmth and spirit to the house. It served another purpose by providing a distraction for her mind after the recent visit from her mother-in-law.

She felt more than just a twinge of guilt for not spending the holidays with them. The Bauer's always enjoyed holiday dinners. She wanted to enjoy those times again, but for now she needed to press forward with the life she was living. She went back into the music room and studied the enormous task in front of her. She decided to take a break and sat at the piano. She often played when Mr. Stafford was not at home. It was a great stress reliever. She was absorbed in playing the classical pieces associated with Christmas when she looked up and saw Brian standing in the doorway. This time he did not startle her, only surprised to see him.

"I did ring the bell this time," he said.

She smiled as she closed the keyboard cover. "I was so engrossed in the music, I didn't hear it. You caught me at one of my guilty pleasures."

He stepped over the mountain of decorations to sit. "I'll be the first to admit I don't know anything about music, but you sounded like a classically trained pianist."

She shrugged. "I was a music major in college, but then my life took a different direction. You never know how things will turn out."

"I assumed you studied to be a chef or something like that," he replied.

She snickered. "It would have been more practical than music. Sometimes one passion demands to take precedence, and it ended up being cooking."

He looked around. "I didn't know Ben had so many decorations, or did Santa's sleigh crash here?"

"It may very well have," she said in a light tone. "I wasn't exactly sure what Mr. Stafford had in the line of decorations, so I dragged them all out. I presumed after our Halloween adventure he might enjoy it if I decorated."

"I'm sure he will. He hasn't bothered in years."

"Too much trouble for a single man?"

Brian hesitated. "Basically. Now for the reason I stopped by; I want to take you to the country club Thanksgiving dinner."

Instantly she became shy and reserved. "I really can't. I have so much to do. I have no idea how long Mr. Stafford will be gone and I wanted to be finished decorating before his return." She remembered something Ben told her. "I thought you have a new girlfriend?"

A hint of a smile crossed Brian's lips. "Had, is the optimum word."

"What happened?" she asked and prepared herself for a ridiculous tale.

"Well," he began and paused. "I took her home one night and then decided to stop by one of my favorite drinking establishments. There was a very pretty and very inebriated young woman. We struck up a conversation and one thing led to another."

Nora rolled her eyes in amusement. There was no remorse in his voice. "How was I supposed to know it was my new girlfriend's sister?"

Nora snorted a laugh. She gleaned enough through casual conversation with her boss to know Brian was less than relationship material.

"You would be doing me a big favor. I don't want to eat alone. The club has a spectacular dinner, not that it compares to one of yours," he was quick to add.

She still did not want to give in, but he seemed so pathetic. "All right, but I don't have much of a wardrobe to pick from for a country club dinner."

He reassured her. "No one will be dressed up, just wear some dress pants and a blouse. I am going just the way I am in my khaki's."

Against her better judgment she agreed, and he said he would pick her up at four. She was not joking when she told him she had nothing to wear. When she left home, she packed only the basics and dresses were not among them. Since she was volunteering at the hospital, she bought a couple pair of dress slacks and sweaters, so she made the most of them. She had no jewelry, not even a simple pair of earrings. She did make the effort to put her hair up and apply the minimal basics of makeup. She never cared about how she looked but she did not want to embarrass Brian, although he was likely impervious to embarrassment. He was too much of a free spirit to worry about others' opinions of him.

She sat nervously in the kitchen waiting for him to arrive and found herself wishing she had not let him talk her into accepting his invitation. She did not belong in society; she was meant to serve it. She knew where she belonged to be comfortable. Soon Brian rapped on the kitchen door before letting himself in. "You look very nice."

"Thank you, Mr. McNair."

He sighed. "For at least today will you please call me Brian. I don't want anyone to think I hired an escort." Then he quickly added, "I mean the legitimate type not the…. well, you know."

Nora laughed at his clumsy attempt to apologize. "Somehow, I do not think anyone will believe you need a professional escort service. If you did, I doubt they would think you'd pick me."

"You underestimate yourself and overestimate the classless group at the country club." He laughed, putting her at ease. She appreciated the compliment; however, she was finding it difficult to make casual conversation. She was not good at small talk, but Brian's mouth never stopped; it was a perfect arrangement.

He pulled up to the port-a-cochere where an eager valet in a red coat helped Nora from the car. Brian took her by the arm guiding her up the stairs and was greeted by the hostess. She directed them to their table as Brian exchanged pleasantries with half the people in the room. When they were seated in a comfortable spot for two near the fireplace he whispered, "Most of the people here are snowbirds waiting to escape to Florida for the winter. They bring their families, so they don't have to cook."

"I suppose that's nice for them," she replied.

"It is like living in a small town when you belong to a country club. Everyone knows everyone's business, which is both good and bad. In the long run I suppose it doesn't matter; they would only make things up anyway."

She was silent because she knew extremely well about everyone knowing her business. That is why she left her hometown. "Do you suppose they are wondering who I am?" she asked with a wary tone glancing around the room.

Brian appeared indifferent. "I doubt it; they have gotten used to me having a date du jour. Don't worry about it."

She was certain he was right and decided to enjoy her evening. It had been a long time since she dined out. As uneasy as she was about accepting Brian's offer, she was now thankful. No matter what chaotic stage her personal life was in, the needs of the inn were consistent. The patrons expected a holiday experience, and one was always given. That need mitigated any crisis, and she allowed herself to enjoy, if not the holiday, the guests' reactions to them. It was now her turn to enjoy the experience.

Brian motioned the waitress over and ordered champagne. They drank a toast to the holiday and a reverent prayer for Ben's mother. Brian said, "Anna is like a mother to me too. My parents died within a year of each other right after my college graduation, and she graciously included me in their family activates. I will be eternally grateful to her for that."

"You don't have any other family?" Nora asked, not entirely certain if she might be crossing a tacit boundary.

"I have a brother, but he is several years older than I and lives in another state. The age difference kept us from being close, not that we don't get along, we're just quite different. What about you?"

A sudden wave of anxiety made her cautious about allowing things to get too personal. "I was an only child. My parents died six years ago too, in a situation similar to yours. They were extremely close, and I honestly think one did not want to live without the other."

He took the champagne from the ice bucket and refilled their glasses. "What did they do for a living?"

"My mother was a substitute librarian for the local school system and taught piano."

"Is that how you learned to play? I knew there must be a musical background in your family for you to be so proficient."

"Yes, but my mother felt I had potential beyond her ability to instruct me, so she pawned me off on a professional music teacher. My father was the manager of the only bank in town, and he also retired from the Air Force Reserve. He was a helicopter pilot in Vietnam."

"That explains your volunteer work at the Veteran's Hospital."

"I try to give back."

He became uncharacteristically solemn. "I envy your parents' relationship. I wish my marriage had been like that. My ex-wife was, or I should say is a good woman, and I didn't appreciate it until I screwed everything up. I realize now she is someone I could have gone the distance with."

"It's the old, woulda, coulda, shoulda, syndrome," she said. "I've been there myself."

"I'm curious, what do you want out of life?"

She did not hesitate because she felt it was a question not intended to be intrusive. "Peace."

"Peace? I was expecting something more tangible."

She nodded. "Yes, you know the kind I am speaking of, where you do all the right things at the right time for the right reasons. When you go to bed at night you don't lie there second guessing yourself."

"Tall order," he said. "If you ever meet a person like that, make sure you introduce me to them. They are like unicorns; I'm afraid they don't exist. Don't you want a husband and children? I think you'd be great at both."

It was obvious Ben did not tell his best friend about the visit from her mother-in-law. She was certain he might allude to it if he knew. She wanted to deflect from anything too personal.

She skillfully brought the subject matter back to him. "I don't have your confidence, but what about you?"

A mischievous grin crossed his lips. "I will make it happen, but not until I grow up."

She giggled. "That could be a while."

He agreed with her pronouncement. "Maybe we will both find what we want."

He did not push her for more details about her life, and she was grateful. He was a complete gentleman and she felt remarkably comfortable in his presence. She believed he was sincere about his regrets at the dissolution of his marriage but found it odd he invited her to Thanksgiving dinner. He was either truly kind or it was an attempt to seduce her. She gave him the benefit of the doubt and chose kindness. She saw no reason to think otherwise. He clearly lacked the self discipline of Ben, but she smiled to herself at his irascible nature. She was certain he was trustworthy and his own worst enemy.

They drank champagne, ate their dinner, and when the band started to play, he asked her to dance. He gracefully guided her around the dance floor. She was not surprised he was such a good dancer; he had an undeniable flare. It was a pleasant evening, and both enjoyed themselves, but it was time for her to return to reality. It was a much-needed diversion for her. When he walked her to the door, she politely thanked him for the lovely evening. She then abruptly stepped inside, closing the door. If Brian had any intention of giving her a goodnight kiss, she did not give him the opportunity.

Chapter Eleven

Wanting the holiday decorating done by the time Ben returned, Nora threw herself into transforming the house. Her urgency had more to do with not wanting to inconvenience him with the mess than it did with the surprise element. It was a consideration too. She decided to concentrate on the areas of the house being used, which consisted of the foyer, Mr. Stafford's library, and the sunroom. She put a few decorations in her quarters as well. He had an extensive collection of cheerful and expensive decorations. She handled them with care, using her skills to make them stand out. She wished she had access to half of his ornaments when she decorated the inn. The only thing she did not find was an artificial Christmas tree, leaving her to assume he bought a fresh one every year. She preferred them herself, however, at the inn when decorating was essential for weeks on end, artificial was the only logical choice. She placed Christmas figurines in the music and living rooms, but they were minimal. She thought one of those rooms was where he'd like to set up a tree so. She placed the box with tree ornaments in the hall closet until she inquired.

Ben arrived early Sunday morning where Nora met him at the door. His first response was similar to when he came home after hiring her. "You made me forget how it used to be decorated. The hallway looks beautiful; I never took the time to attach garlands to the staircase. You certainly have an eye for detail. I feel festive already and I can use a little of that right now. You have been so busy it's highly unlikely you took any time off."

"This is enjoyable for me. Even if you aren't in a holiday mood it's pretty hard not to enjoy colored lights."

"That is the truth. If you are fortunate enough to have pleasant childhood memories, Christmas is the time of year to help you remember," he said as he continued to look around.

Nora asked, "How is Mrs. Stafford?"

"Better than I expected. She was able to have Thanksgiving dinner with us. Libby did everything, and for once Mom was able to sit back and enjoy it. She was incredibly lucky; they called it a mini stroke. Did you celebrate at all?"

"Mr. McNair took me the country club for dinner."

He was silent and a scowl froze on his face. Nora instantly discerned he did not approve. "Was I out of line? I didn't want to go, but he was so insistent and a little pathetic about not wanting to be alone. Things did not work out with his girlfriend. A reason to decline his kind offer didn't occur to me quick enough."

Ben shook his head and gave a dismissive wave of his hand. "I'm sorry, I didn't mean to give you the impression you shouldn't have accepted. As much as I love Brian, he is pretty reckless with women's feelings. I do not want you to be hurt by him. He sometimes doesn't think beyond what he wants in the moment."

"Oh no, it was nothing like that, it was just dinner. I am aware of his reputation no matter how likeable he is. I was alone and he was alone, I am still a little uncomfortable about it. It wasn't very professional of me."

"Don't be sorry, and it's none of my business. Of course, you need to socialize, and I am in the wrong to make you feel otherwise. It's Brian's motives which concern me."

****

It may not have been any of his business, but he was furious with Brian and wasted no time contacting him. He asked him to meet him at the village diner. Ben was tapping his fingers on the table as he waited for Brian to join him. Soon he sauntered through the door and asked, "How's Anna?"

Ben snapped at him. "She is fine. Forget about my mother. What were you thinking taking Nora to the country club for Thanksgiving?"

Brian stared at him in stunned silence before asking, "What's wrong with that? Aren't I supposed to mix with the hired help?"

Ben pounded his fist on the table causing his water glass to rattle. "She is too *good* for you. Don't mess with her, please. She will be fun for you for a while and then you'll cheat on her just like you always do. She is too kind of a person for your antics and may very well leave."

Brian grinned as he leaned back in his chair. "Ahh, that's the real rub, isn't it? You are afraid of losing someone who keeps you all nice and orderly, so you don't have to risk actually living your life."

Ben bent over the table and spoke in a harsh whisper, "I've lived it."

Brian replied with compassion in his voice, "I lived

it with you. We only go around once, Ben. Life goes on whether you want it to or not, so go with it. For what it's worth, I was a total gentleman and honestly just wanted to have the pleasure of her company for dinner. She was the quintessential Nora and left no room for anything other than dinner. Although I admit she intrigues me."

Ben was relieved. Brian often frustrated him, but he always told the truth. "Just lay off her, okay?"

Brian reached over and gave Ben a pat on the shoulder. "You're right about her being too good for me, nearly every woman is. She isn't likely to give me the time of day, but if she did, I can't make you any promises."

****

The middle of December had arrived, and Nora decided to ask if Ben wanted a Christmas tree. She knocked on his library door and asked, "Sir, were you going to buy a tree? It was the only thing I did not find among the decorations in the basement."

He clicked off his computer screen to give her his full attention. "I haven't decorated in many years. I was so engrossed with everything you've done I completely forgot about a tree. Sure, why not? Do you want to help me pick it out? We could go on Saturday. I'm sure you have a better eye for that kind of thing than I."

On Saturday they drove his SUV to a Christmas tree lot in the village of Bartholomew. It grew extremely cold and began snowing, but it did not deter them. Nora picked through them like a surgeon during an operation but finally she chose one. "This is it," she proudly proclaimed.

Ben walked around it appearing to give it the same

scrutiny Nora did and asked, "How do you know? They all seem to look the same to me."

Nora clutched at her heart to feign an attack. "That is sacrilege to say; all trees are not created equal. The right one sets the stage for all the decorations."

He bowed to her. "Excuse me, I was not aware I was in the presence of the tree goddess."

They both began to laugh and shared in a moment of intimacy previously not experienced between them. After their selection, the lot attendant tossed it through the machine which wrapped it tightly in plastic mesh and tied it to the roof of the car.

Once they arrived home, Ben pulled into the garage and Nora helped him take it off the roof. He was about to carry it into the house until Nora stopped him. "It's best if we leave it in here for the night to acclimate to the temperature difference. I will set it up tomorrow."

"You'll need help. It's rather heavy and awkward to do it alone."

She did not expect any difficulty doing it herself, but he was right. It was easier with two people, so she accepted his offer of help. The next morning Ben brought the tree stand up from the basement and carried the tree into the music room. He placed it in the stand and held it upright while Nora turned the screws into the tree trunk. When they were certain it was straight, Ben cut the plastic netting to allow the tree to spread. Instantly the house filled with the pleasant aroma of freshly cut pine. Ben took a deep breath. "No smell quite like it, is there?"

"I agree. It isn't Christmas until you can smell the pine boughs. At the inn it was necessary to decorate with artificial trees and greenery. I went to a local

Christmas tree farm where the owner let me take the trimmings. They had a pile of branches trimmed off the bottom of the trees, so I brought them to the inn and placed them in baskets around the rooms. If they dried out, I replaced them. At least we always had the scent of natural pine." She stepped back to look at the tree adding, "We should let the branches drop a bit before we start to decorate."

Admiring the fullness of the tree he said, "I've forgotten about all the idiosyncrasies of putting up a tree."

Nora pulled the box of tree ornaments from the hall closet and they sat on the floor taking them out one by one. They checked for any which may have broken over the years. Nora was laying them on the floor in order of size and color. Ben seemed to have embraced the ritual when she saw him take something from the box. He suddenly got up, left the room, and went directly into his library where he uncharacteristically closed the door. Whatever he took obviously upset him.

About an hour later he appeared and told her he was going out for a while and not to bother cooking dinner for him. He looked so sad and somber she began to worry about him. When he came home a couple of hours later, he went directly to his bedroom and didn't appear for the rest of the evening. She finished decorating the tree alone and put the leftover ornaments back in the basement.

The following morning Ben did not come down for breakfast. He was a man who kept a predictable routine, so the concern she had for him the previous night, mounted. Finally, at eight o'clock she went upstairs to his room and gently knocked on the door. He did not answer. She knocked a little louder, she heard unintelligible mumbling. Her worry escalated as she entered his room. His bedroom or Ben reeked of whiskey. He was slouched in a chair near the window with a glass on the floor tipped over and a bottle of whiskey on the end table next to him. Dangling from his finger was a Christmas tree ornament made from construction paper with sparkling glitter on it. It had a pipe cleaner stuck through the paper to be used to hang from a tree branch. It was the obvious work of a child. Nora knelt beside him, gently shaking his arm. "Mr. Stafford, are you ill? May I help you?"

His glassy eyes opened, he looked at her troubled face, and then spotted the ornament dangling from his finger. He jumped to his feet sliding it between the cushion and arm of his chair. "I'm fine; what time is it?"

"After eight. When you didn't come to breakfast, I was afraid you were ill."

"I'm feeling poorly, but I'm afraid it is of my own making. I have to get to the office. Just put coffee in a travel mug for me."

As she left the bedroom, she heard his shower turn on followed by the unmistakable sounds of retching. She returned to the kitchen where she filled the coffee mug. She busied herself in another room, allowing him to discreetly leave without further embarrassment. After he left, she went to clean up his room. While she was hanging up his clothes, she noticed the attic door ajar. It had never been open before, and she had no occasion to explore its contents. She flicked on the light and headed up the stairs. It was a typical attic, unfinished storage space with miscellaneous items of postponed disposal.

What she was surprised to see was a rocking chair pulled up alongside a dismantled crib and boxes of toys. Next to the chair was another whiskey glass and when she picked it up it still held a small amount of liquid. She theorized he was sitting there last night. A picture was emerging, and it deeply saddened her. His behavior allowed her to assume he had lost a child. The photo she saw him looking at from his wallet might have been his daughter. Where there was a child, there must be a mother. As curious as she might be, she respected his privacy as he did hers.

When he returned home later that afternoon he behaved as if nothing was different and even stopped to admire the tree. "You did a wonderful job on it. It is beautiful."

Nora took his coat from him, hanging it in the closet. Assuming his stomach was still weak, she used the same diplomacy of the morning. "Thank you, I hope it meets with your approval. I am very sorry I lost track of time and didn't make your refreshments."

"I think I will skip them today. In fact, I'd like a bowl of soup and a dinner roll served in my library and nothing more."

She prepared homemade chicken soup, placed it on a tray with a couple of buttered rolls and a large glass of club soda with a fresh lemon wedge. She sat it on his desk. He looked at her with tacit gratitude, nothing needed to be said. She saw him taking a couple of spoons of soup, likely waiting to see if it stayed down, and then smiled. She placed two aspirins under his roll, which he found and instantly dispatched with a gulp of soda. Satisfied he was well, Nora returned to the kitchen.

****

Christmas was only three days away when Ben interrupted Nora in the middle of preparing breakfast. "Do you have any plans for Christmas Eve?"

She shrugged. "Not really. I'll probably watch an old movie on TV."

"I thought you'd probably say that, so Brian and I want you to join us for Christmas Eve dinner."

She was reluctant when asked to join them. "What do you want me to prepare?"

He laughed. "You are not going to prepare anything; you will be our guest for a change. I have already placed an order with Henri's to cater it. Brian will pick up the food and bring it here."

"The little French restaurant on Main Street?"

"That's the one. The food is wonderful," he said adding, "but nothing compares to yours, of course."

"I have read the reviews and heard nothing but praise for them. I can hardly refuse. I will consider it research."

Ben had a bemused expression on his face. "Interesting way to look at a holiday dinner."

Nora giggled. "I'm sorry if I sound ungrateful; I'll be looking forward to it."

On Christmas Eve, Nora set the dining room table with the best China, silver, crystal, and linens. It was a pleasure to have such grand things to work with, and she had the ability to make the table shine. Ben went into his wine cellar and brought out a couple bottles of his best wine before Brian arrived with the food. Everything was perfect. After dinner Ben suggested they go into the music room to enjoy a brandy and dessert. Nora slowly sipped her drink, she rarely indulged in alcohol, unlike her hosts. Finally, Brian said, "Nora, why don't you play something in keeping with the season." Ben's eyebrows formed a curious expression as he watched Nora go to the piano. "Didn't you know she has been commandeering your piano?"

"No, and I'm more surprised you did?"

She started playing a classical version of "Oh Holy Night," and Ben was mesmerized. With genuine appreciation in his voice he said, "I had no idea you played the piano. Please feel free to play when I am home; you don't have to hide your talent."

"Thank you, but it is just something I do to take a break. I didn't think you'd mind—" And then giving a reproving look to Brian. "—and frankly I didn't think you'd ever find out. Mr. McNair walked in on me on Thanksgiving Day and my secret was out."

She played a few more carols, then Ben said, "I have a gift for you." He handed her an envelope and inside was a gift certificate for a prestigious day salon which included lunch. "My secretary assured me every woman she knows loves it. Take a day off and do those girly things women like to do."

It was a very extravagant gift. She knew the place by reputation and there was often a waiting list to get an appointment. "I don't know what to say. I know I will enjoy it."

Next, Brian presented her with a small box, when she opened it there was a simple but elegant gold chain necklace. "It's lovely, thank you." She ignored the reproving look Ben gave him. Jewelry was considered too personal a gift for a casual friendship.

"It so happens I have something for you two as well," she said reaching under the sofa to produce two packages. One she handed to Brian. He opened it and started to laugh. It was an engraved keychain. "It's for your housekey," she said. He pulled the key to Ben's front door from his pocket and promptly attached it.

Ben opened his gift; it was a gardening book. "The bookstore clerk told me the pictures and garden plans are specifically designed for this region." He started to flip the pages and was so engrossed in it he almost forgot to thank her. She was pleased she found him the perfect gift.

"What are everyone's plans for tomorrow?" Brian asked.

"I will be at the Veteran's Hospital," she said. "It is a lonely time for many of the patients."

"I will be having dinner with my office manager's family. They always take pity on me and invite me every year," Ben replied.

"And I'll be at my ex-wife's," Brian said. "It's nice to visit my old house and dog once in a while."

Ben laughed. "I'm sure the dog will be happier to see you than Molly."

Chapter Twelve

On Christmas morning Nora rose early, and brewed a pot of coffee for Ben before he came downstairs. She was more than willing to make him breakfast, but she did not know what he might want to eat. He may skip breakfast considering he was going out to Christmas dinner. When he came into the kitchen, he seemed surprised to see her. "I thought you might be gone by now to volunteer at the hospital," he said as he reached for the coffee pot.

"I will shortly, but I was waiting for you to check if you want me to make you something. I am not sure I am up to the same standards as Henri's, but I'll try."

"I will take your cooking over his any time," Ben said. "Don't worry about me. It's Christmas, so have fun. You get back when you get back. The veterans need you more than I do. This must be a particularly lonely time of year for those without families."

She poured coffee into a travel mug before heading for the door. "Have an enjoyable time, sir. When I return, I will cook dinner if you like."

"Nora," he said in a stern voice. "I told you this is a holiday. No doubt I will be sent home with plenty of leftovers. I already stuffed myself more than necessary with last night's feast."

With a nod, she headed for her car. There was little traffic on the snow-covered roads; she assumed everyone must be at home opening presents. She was surprised there were so many cars in the parking lot of the hospital as she pulled into an open space. When she opened the entrance doors, she could hear carolers singing. She recognized many of them as fellow volunteers. She smiled as a large group of patients in their wheelchairs gathered around the enormous grand piano, singing at the top of their and lungs practically drowning out the carolers.

Nora's heart skipped a beat when she saw a young woman holding a baby and realized it was Christa. The young woman spotted her and approached with a broad smile. "Merry Christmas. It's so good to see you again."

"Is everything okay? You and the baby why are you here?" she asked realizing it was an intrusive question to ask. She was so stunned to see her it frightened her.

"My husband is a patient," she said without any clear distress in her voice.

Christa's answer did little to assuage her concern. "Oh, no! Was he wounded?"

Christa laughed as she bounced the baby up and down. "I suppose you could call it that. When he returned home from overseas, I was picking him up at the base when another soldier accidently ran over his foot."

Nora laughed with her although it certainly was not funny but vastly different from her first thought. "How bad is it?"

Still smiling she said, "It's not too bad, but they did some minor surgery on his foot; it's why he's here."

"Probably not the Christmas you thought you'd

celebrate," Nora replied.

Christa was now somber. "Any Christmas where he is safe on United States soil is a Christmas to celebrate."

In a quiet voice Nora said, "I couldn't agree with you more."

"Do you want to hold the baby?" Christa asked but thrust the child into her arms before she answered.

Nora took the little bundle and held the baby against her chest. "Boy or girl?"

"It's a boy, Ian Robert O'Reilly," she said with pride.

Smiling down at the child Nora said softly, "Welcome to the world, Ian, you certainly have a nice mommy." With that she handed him back to his mother.

Christa placed a pacifier in his mouth. "Do you have any children?"

It was the most personal question anyone had asked her since arriving in town and she hesitated before replying. "No, no I was never blessed." Then, to Nora's relief, Christa was called away by her husband.

A nurse who was checking on the elderly patients approached. "I'm so glad you made it. Mr. Pirelli is asking for you."

"He's not down here with the others?" she asked, looking around knowing he loved a good party.

"No, he has not been feeling well lately but I know he'd love to see you. He asked if you were here."

His status as a World War II veteran and her unofficial *boyfriend* gave her a reason for concern. "Of course, how bad is he?"

"He's holding his own, but he's too weak to be brought down here for the festivities."

She shook her head. "That's a shame. No one enjoys a party like Vincent."

"I can have an extra tray of dinner sent up to his room if you'd like to dine with him. I know he would appreciate the company."

"I'd be honored," Nora said and headed for the elevator.

Vincent Pirelli had a private room on the top floor with one of the best views of the hospital grounds. He was a kind and caring old man who faded in an out of reality. He had lived at the hospital for so long she guessed the administrator gave him the prime room for just that reason. She never saw anyone visit him. She wondered if he had any family, and if he did, where were they at Christmas?

When Nora entered the room, his face lit up. "I've got my very own Christmas angel."

She went to his bedside and gave him a kiss on the cheek. "Merry Christmas, Mr. Pirelli."

"I told you to call me Vinny; we've known each other for decades." His tone was playful and light.

She was never sure whether he believed it or not, but she always went along with him. "My mother told me to address a gentleman as Mr."

He giggled childishly. "That's your first mistake; who ever said I was a gentleman?"

She gave his hand a gentle squeeze. "You are the most gentlemanly person I ever met." She was sincere. He may make an occasional frisky comment, but he never crossed the line of propriety no matter how far his mind slipped.

"The nurse said she will bring my dinner so we can celebrate Christmas together," she told him and then pulled a bottle of sparkling wine from her tote bag. She asked for permission to bring the wine. Not a single doctor objected to him having a festive drink with his special lady.

The twinkle came back into his eyes. "I see what you're doing; you are wining and dining me to gain access to my walker."

Feigning fear of discovery she replied, "I thought I was going to get away with it; you're too clever for me. Is your wheelchair up for grabs?"

He shook his head and reached out to touch her hand. "You don't want it; the wheels squeak."

Nora felt like her old self when she was visiting with Vincent. She became the warm and amusing person she used to be because she did not need to have her guard up. She set the small table in his room by the window so they could eat and enjoy the view. When the trays of turkey with all the trimming arrived, she helped him into his wheelchair to sit next to her. He told her about the *good old days* of his childhood. They were as clear in his mind as if they were yesterday. He spoke of his parents and his beautiful sister. It sounded as if he had an idyllic childhood, despite living through the Great Depression. He regaled her with stories of growing up on a nearby farm. He laughed when he told her the Depression meant little to them because they were already poor. The farm gave them everything they needed, and they fared better than most. He never mentioned a wife or children, and apart from brief references, he did not speak of the war.

"How about you, child?" he asked during their meal.

"What do you mean?" she asked not knowing if he

was living in the present, past, or something imaginary.

"Are you happy? Do you have a family to share this day? Certainly, as charming as I know I am, you would prefer a more eventful Christmas."

She replied in a flirty tone. "I'm shocked you'd say such a thing. What is more eventful than a day with you?"

After they finished their meal, he began to nod off. She rang for the nurse, and they helped him back into his bed. As she pulled the blankets up, he smiled and patted her hand. "Thank you from a grateful old man."

She gave him a kiss on the cheek. "It's been my pleasure."

It may not have been the most exciting Christmas for Nora, but it was one of the most meaningful ones she ever celebrated. There was so much courage, not just with Mr. Pirelli, but with the other patients as well. They had experienced unimageable horrors, but they were survivors. Her heart broke for those, like Vincent, who had no one to share their burdens.

****

Brian was having a different type of Christmas with his ex-wife Molly and the dog. He and Molly had been divorced for three years but somehow remained friends. Brian was the most affable person on the face of the earth and made friends everywhere he went. It was what caused many of his problems. When he got too friendly, Molly gave him his marching orders. It was a testament to their relationship they not only remained civil but occasionally spent time together. He pathetically appealed to her kind nature to impose himself on her for the holiday.

Brian made himself comfortable in his old home.

He threw a couple logs on the fire, made himself a drink, and stretched out on the sofa with the dog. Molly stood in front of him, hands on her hips, and said, "Don't get too comfortable, you are a guest not a resident."

He reached out, grabbed her arm, and pulled her onto the sofa next to him. "Admit it, you love having me here. It's just like old times."

"I will have you know I had to lie to my parents and brothers to get out of dinner with them. If they had the slightest notion you were here, they'd slap me silly. You are not one of their favorite people."

He slipped his hand under her shirt and asked playfully, "Then why did you do it?"

"Because I'm a sentimental idiot. Don't you have a girlfriend for the holidays? God knows you have enough of them during the rest of year."

"Tsk, tsk, tsk," he muttered. "You want me here, admit it."

She yanked his hand from under her shirt, changing the topic to a safer subject. "So, Ben finally found a cook who didn't quit at the first chance?"

Brian sat up and grabbed his drink. "They are the strangest pair."

She smiled and asked, "What do you mean?"

"They have this exaggerated formality between them. They hardly ever speak more than a sentence or two at a time to each other, and she calls him *sir*."

Molly had just taken a sip of her drink and nearly spit it back into the glass. "Granted Ben doesn't wear his heart on his sleeve, but he's not into the *Lord of the manor* thing. I know why he lives that way, but why would she?"

He tossed a ball across the room and the dog ran after it while he explained. "I have no idea; it's weird, but it works. This is the most relaxed I have seen him in years. He isn't the old Ben but a much better version than I've seen in a long time."

Molly leaned forward in anticipation of a tidbit of gossip. "Is there something between them?"

Brian laughed. "Yes, a dust mop. What I mean is, he has the peace of mind that all the loose ends of his life are tidied up. His house is immaculate, I mean you literally could eat off the floor. She is a gourmet cook and tends to the things he doesn't even know he needs."

Molly giggled. "She sounds perfect for you."

A sly grin crossed his lips. "It crossed my mind, but you would have to know her to understand why she wouldn't touch me with a ten-foot pole. Ben told me she was too good for me."

"Most women are. You tried to hit on her, didn't you?"

"I'd be insulted if it wasn't true," he joked as he made another drink. "But seriously, I feel better knowing she is in the house with him, and I think she needs the distraction too. She is quite shy and introverted. She is hiding away as much as he is, probably not for the same reason."

"Ben has to let go of his pain at some point. It's not healthy for him."

Brian defended his friend, but also agreed with his ex-wife. "You can't tell a person to just 'snap out of it,' they have to heal when they're ready."

They listened to some holiday music and, just when he was about to make a move, she said, "It's getting late. Time for you to go."

He gave her his best puppy dog eye look. She laughed as she pulled him to his feet, threw his coat at him, and said, "Good night, Brian."

****

Ben was grateful to his office manager for dutifully inviting him every year for dinner, but he would rather stay at home. The Bishops were a wonderful, close-knit family and genuinely made him feel like he was an important guest, but his quiet nature was a contrast to their exuberance. The children ran around the house playing with their new toys, shouting, and screaming as children do, especially at Christmas. He thought about the sanctity of his library, a glass of bourbon, and soft music playing. Christmas just did not have the same meaning to him any longer, but he honored it in his own way.

He stayed through dinner, had dessert and coffee, and then politely thanked them before leaving. He seldom stayed past dessert, so they made no attempt to ask him to stay. It was enough for him to know they cared to include him in their family holiday traditions. He was home before Nora and intended on doing just as he was dreaming of, having a drink in his library. He made a bourbon but wandered to the Christmas tree and sat on the sofa staring at it. It had been years since the house was decorated, and it made him feel hopeful just as Christmas was intended. He was not a changed man; his wounds were too deep. But he wanted to change and that was the first step.

Suddenly, he wondered if Nora had similar feelings. Was all her festive decorating out of habit or hope? He was beginning to want to know more, but at the same time he was afraid to reveal too much of himself. He heard her come through the kitchen entrance and sought her out to ask about her day. She looked up after removing her boots. "How was your dinner?"

He absently rattled the ice cubes in his drink. "Very nice. They are a good family and the kids, although loud and rambunctious, are very respectful and well behaved."

Her smile showed a glint in her eyes. "Just like when your family were here, it was nice to have them but nice to see them go?"

A guilty grin crossed his lips. "Something like that."

"Well, it is Christmas; kids are over stimulated and full of energy. I imagine your niece is enjoying her first Christmas back in the States. Did you speak with Mrs. Stafford?"

He nodded. "I called them on my way home. My sister's husband has joined them, and all his business is wrapped up in Sweden. His parents drove over to my mother's house where my sister is temporarily living. It sounds as if they are having a real family Christmas."

"Do you wish you were there?"

He cocked his head to one side, momentarily staring up at the ceiling in thought and said, "Maybe just a little, but not enough to actually travel there." He changed the subject and asked, "How was your day?"

She sat down at the kitchen island and sighed. "It was…meaningful. There are three groups of patients: the ones ready to leave, the ones too seriously injured to care about Christmas, and the forgotten or alone ones. I spent my Christmas dining with my boyfriend."

He knew she was speaking of the veteran she

befriended. "I think it's very kind of you to help him."

She shook her head. "It's not kindness, it's not even duty. He is a really nice old man who should have a dozen grandchildren to spoil."

"He doesn't have anyone?"

"I'm afraid not. A nurse once told me he was a widower, but beyond that I don't know anything about him. He is very friendly, but I suspect he has outlived his close friends and now he is alone."

Ben nodded; he knew what it was to be alone.

"Did you want me to make you something to eat before I go to my room?"

He put his hands in the air in a surrender gesture. "Good heavens, no! If I eat one more thing I will explode. I just wanted to check on your Christmas."

"Thank you. Will you be going into the office in the morning?"

"Yes, not much gets done between Christmas and New Year's, but I have some financials to get in order. I gave my staff vacation until after the New Year."

Their brief exchange of pleasantries ended, and they returned to their impersonal employer/employee personas.

Chapter Thirteen

Nora was relieved the rest of the holiday season went smoothly. It was completely uneventful, exactly what she wanted. For too many years there was drama in her life, especially when the holidays rolled around. It made her sad when she finally took down the decorations. For several days, the house felt empty and lonely without them, however she did like the clean minimalistic look. She never found the ornament Ben hid in his bedroom chair. She assumed he must have found a special place for it.

Unfortunately, the end of Christmas did not mean the end of the snow. Nora enjoyed the winters and its snowfalls, but it had more to do with bringing ambiance for the holidays. When they were over so was her enthusiasm for snow. It was shaping up to be a brutal winter not just with snow accumulation, but bitter cold as well. To make matters worse, Ben received a phone call of an unpleasant nature. Nora heard him say with disgust, "Nooo, please don't tell me that." He put the receiver down and stood staring as if he hoped it might ring again with better news.

"Something wrong?" she asked.

His face was distorted with anguish. "That was the State Police; they said my cabin was broken into and trashed."

"I didn't know you had a cabin. I don't think you

ever mentioned it."

"I haven't been there in a couple of years. It's about fifty miles northeast of here in the woods on a small lake. It's nothing fancy, but it does have water and electricity. The lake is perfect for swimming and fishing. My grandfather built a dock for us to dive off and have access to the lake in the winter to ice skate. There are no motorboats allowed, only canoes. It keeps it serene and natural. The most use it gets now is from Brian for his trysts, and sometimes people from my office go for a weekend. I'd drag Brian up there with me to see what needs being done, but he went away for the weekend."

Nora was wiping down the countertops when she asked, "Is it something I can help you with?"

"I couldn't ask you to do that, besides, I don't know how bad it is."

"It really doesn't matter whether I'm working here or there. Between the two of us we can clean it up and assess the damage."

He pulled out a counter stool and dropped heavily on it. "I'd really appreciate any help you can give me. We will have to spend the night if we want to get everything done."

"I'll pack warm. Do you have cleaning supplies?"

He waved his hand. "I honestly do not know what's there. The people I let use it do so with the understanding they keep it clean. My guests may have brought cleaning things with them."

She shrugged. "You really don't need much more than bleach and a good dish soap. I can put together something from here to take and pack any food we will need. You do have dishes and such, don't you?"

"There always used to be, but again I don't know what may have been taken or destroyed. The Trooper said he secured the door, but it is only a temporary fix. It was a neighbor who spotted it ajar and called them. I got lucky because usually few people go there in the winter."

The snow was persistent in its accumulation leaving no question they needed the four-wheel drive of his SUV. Nora packed her supplies and food and threw in extra blankets and bed linens just to cover all their bases. They only intended to be gone for one night.

"Do you have any tools?"

He grinned. "This may surprise you, but I do, and I know how to use them."

She was surprised but not rude enough to tell him so. He packed his tool kit with boxes of nails and screws. "I hope this will be sufficient to fix the damage. I won't rest until I see for myself."

They left as soon as they packed. The streets around the house were still in good condition but the winding mountain roads near the cabin were treacherous. They were snow covered and slippery which turned an hour drive into a two-hour drive. Ben's SUV plowed through the drifts to the front door of the cabin. The State Trooper's tire marks were still visible but rapidly disappearing in the snow. Nora stepped from the car into a deep drift, nearly toppling over. Her mouth opened but she was speechless at first. "This is everything you expect when someone tells you they have a cabin."

It was a small flat logged building with chinking in between the logs. The roof extended both in the front and back to cover porches. The boards creaked as they crossed over them to the front door. The door frame had been pried open allowing the burglars to gain entry.

"Given the remote location I'm surprised this hasn't happened sooner," Ben said. He removed the Trooper's make-shift lock, opened the door, and turned on the lights. "I suppose it might be worse."

The cabin, trashed for pure vandalism, not theft, eluded comprehension. "If they wanted anything in here, why didn't they just take it? What pleasure is there in destroying everything?" Ben asked out loud. The furniture was tipped over, dishes broken, the television thrown to the floor, DVDs stomped on, and ashes and logs from the fireplace strewn around. Even with the mess, Nora could easily visualize its charm. It consisted of one large room with a modest bathroom. It included a toilet, sink, and shower, not elaborate, but serviceable. The only other room was an upstairs sleeping loft.

Ben kicked aside the broken items as glass crunched beneath his feet. His tone was weary. "Brian was the last person here and thankfully he shut off the water main. If the pipes froze or the burglars turned on the faucets, the place might be a total loss. I don't even know where to begin."

"With a large garbage bag and broom. You don't want to get cut on all this glass," Nora warned. As she swept up the broken dishes, Ben up righted the furniture and brought in their supplies. He made a temporary repair to the door jamb allowing them to lock the door. He cleaned out the fireplace and started a fire. The cabin had a damp, musty smell but a little heat fixed the problem. By the time they finished, they had six large contractor bags filled with garbage. While Ben dragged them out on the porch, Nora wiped her hands on the seat of her pants. "What a waste."

"Thank goodness they didn't slit the leather furniture or spray paint the walls," he said.

Working together, the worst of it was cleaned up in a few hours. Nora then completed a deeper cleaning because it had gone unused for an extended period of time.

"There's a little diner in the village if you'd like to get something to eat," Ben suggested.

"I brought food; I'll cook."

Ben reached for his car keys on the counter. "No, you have worked too hard. We'll go grab something in town." After they put on their coats and opened the door, they discovered it had snowed so hard while they worked the car was now invisible. "Like I said," he chortled. "Why don't you cook something?"

She laughed as he closed the door. It was pleasant with the fire burning; neither of them seemed to mind remaining in the quaint cabin. "This sofa folds out to a comfortable bed. Why don't you take the loft upstairs. It will give you more privacy," he suggested.

"It really doesn't matter. I can sleep down here."

"I am not confident with my door repair. I'd rather you sleep upstairs."

Nora's eyes opened wide. "Do you think the burglars will come back?"

"It's not likely, especially in this weather, but better safe than sorry."

The food Nora brought was leftovers from the freezer at home. She defrosted them in the microwave, which had been spared from abuse because it was mounted to the wall. The electric range was also operational, allowing her to finish the meal. In such a small space the aroma of food quickly filled the cabin. While it was heating Nora reached inside the cooler they brought. "I snagged a couple bottles of your favorite wine. I thought you might need it."

He was giddy as he grabbed the bottle from her. "That's an understatement, but you'll have to join me." He clutched the bottle neck staring at the cork. "Do we have a way of opening it, not to mention something to pour it in?"

"The silverware, of course didn't break, and I think I spotted a corkscrew."

She rifled through the drawers, found one, along with plastic plates and cups at the back of a lower cupboard. "We're in business."

Ben poured them each a glass as they sat before the fire waiting for their food to cook. He raised his glass touching hers. "To your health."

She smiled and scanned the room. "The cabin is so quaint. I cannot imagine why you haven't been here in such a long time. What a relaxing place to reflect and regroup."

Ben leaned back onto the sofa with a distant look in his eyes. "My grandfather and my father built this place with their own two hands when my dad was a kid."

"Really? All the more reason it is special."

He continued reminiscing. "We spent summers here as kids. Swimming, fishing, boating; name it, we did it. When my sister became a teenager and was more into boys and makeup, she lost interest in the place. Dad and I still came up here frequently for a little male bonding. He died the next day at home after one of the best weekends we ever shared."

There was no sadness in his voice, in fact only tranquility. She nodded. "Bittersweet?"

He looked at her as if he were seeing her for the first time. "I couldn't have put it any better. He was dying, and we all knew he did not have much time left. I think our weekend was meant as his gift to me. We talked about everything. We laughed, we cried, and even dared to dream. He was the wisest person I knew. One of his favorite expressions was 'never judge a man until you walk a mile in his shoes.' He was more tolerant than I, but I think about that often and try to emulate him. He left the cabin to me, and sitting here talking about it makes me ashamed I haven't tried to get back to what's really important." Then he turned to Nora and asked his first personal question. "What about your childhood?"

She had so carefully avoided speaking of herself ever since she started working for him, she did not mind answering his question because it was not meant as intrusive. "Not really unlike yours, except I was an only child. My parents were great, and naturally they doted on me because they were much older than most first-time parents. They died years ago. You never stop missing them."

He shook his head with sadness. "No, you don't."

Nora broke the silence which had fallen when she jumped to her feet. "I think dinner is done."

She put the pots directly on the table to serve themselves. Bowls had been a casualty of the vandalism, but it was still difficult to think of it as *roughing it*. They had heat, water, electricity, and a sturdy roof over their heads for shelter. After they ate,

Ben insisted upon doing all the dishes and cleaning up. Nora protested but he didn't let her lift a finger. When he finished, he poured a little more wine into a glass and handed it to her. "Just sit here and keep warm; you've earned it."

She wrapped a blanket around her shoulders. "It is still a little chilly in here."

He picked up a fireplace poker, stoked the fire, and tossed in a couple more logs. "That's because it is not insulated like a traditional house. The logs are thick and will protect from the cold, but it takes longer for them to absorb the heat. By morning it will be toasty."

"Just in time to leave," Nora said with a sigh.

He shrugged. "Yea, probably."

****

Nora dozed off on the sofa; it may have been the early darkness of winter or all the work she did, but she was clearly exhausted. As Ben did not have the heart to wake her, he decided to let her sleep. He was not tired; his mind was too full of nostalgic thoughts. Most of them were pleasant like the memories he shared with Nora, but others were not.

He poured himself the last of the wine and shook the bottle wishing it might magically refill. He drank it slowly as he meandered around the small room. His hand slid across the hand-hewn fireplace mantle. He smiled as he remembered as children, he and Libby hung Christmas stockings, and worried Santa might get burnt. He turned his gaze out the window, unable to tell if it was still snowing or if the wind was whipping it around. It occurred to him they might find themselves stranded; a consideration he did not find unpleasant. It was the first time in a long time he let himself explore all the things he had every right to be grateful for, and for too long denied. When tragedy and challenging times find people, it is easy to forget as terrible things come so eventually do good.

He sat in the armchair next to the fireplace and watched Nora sleep. She looked so peaceful. Countless times, he looked into her eyes, and she seemed as though she was scared and wanted to bolt. No one as kind and loyal as she should ever feel that way. It was for that reason, he wished he knew more about her. He lived with his own pain for so long, he was aware of how it transformed a person. He was starting to feel as though he was at a healing point. He was not sure why he felt that way, but he did. He hoped Nora was heading in the same direction. She was guarded about everything she said and did; he felt certain she was not there yet. Talking about her childhood gave him insight into her background. She had the same happy, secure childhood he enjoyed. It may not have prepared them for hardships to come, but it was a solid foundation to getting through them. For some people, the journey is longer than others.

****

Nora woke from her nap and was momentarily disoriented. She looked over and saw Ben had also nodded off. His feet were up on the footstool and his head drooped down on his chest. She did not want to disturb him for the same reason he did not want to wake her; he seemed content.

She pulled the cushions off the sofa and stacked them in the corner as she opened it to unfold the bed. She made it up with the blankets and linens she brought and then did the same thing for herself with a bed in the loft. She was not sure about waking him, but she thought a good night's sleep on the sofa bed was preferable to a neck spasm from sleeping in the chair. She gently shook his arm.

"Mr. Stafford, I made up your bed."

He rubbed his eyes and sleepily staggered toward the sofa bed. He kicked off his shoes, climbed in with all his clothes still on, and was back asleep again before Nora reached the loft. She paused on the stairs smiling when she heard him snoring.

Neither of them woke early, but Nora made it to the kitchen area just as he started to stir. "Wow!" he exclaimed. "I forgot how quiet it is here."

"I slept well myself. How does the weather look outside?" She was thinking about the drive back home.

He went over to the window and drew back the curtain. "Not bad, at least it isn't snowing. I hope we can get to the main road. The SUV is dependable. After breakfast I will see if I can make a path with it. No point in packing up and dragging stuff to the car if we can't get out. Do we have any coffee?"

"Yep," she said lightly. "But the coffeemaker was one of the causalities. I think I can boil water and drip it through the filter. It won't be perfect, but it will be coffee."

"Anything will be great."

They ate the eggs Nora brought with leftover steak from the freezer. Ben was now feeling energized. "I'll take a try at making some tracks with the car if you want to shower. I will take my turn when I get back."

She was feeling grungy after cleaning up the mess from yesterday, so she quickly took advantage of his absence. She had just gotten dressed when he returned looking like a snowman. He stomped the snow off his feet and brushed his coat before removing it. "It was ugly, but I made it. We'll be able to get home. I already loaded up the garbage."

"If you don't mind, I'd like to look around outside while you're getting cleaned up. It seems so picturesque."

"Help yourself." He grabbed his clean clothes from the overnight bag and headed for the bathroom.

She bundled up and trekked around the outside of the cabin. If she had not known there was a lake out back, she might have assumed it was a snow-covered meadow. It was frozen solid because she saw children ice skating far off in the distance. There was a steep hill nearby making her wonder if Ben and his sister tobogganed down it as kids. She clearly understood why he never parted with the place even if he did not make full use of it. She must have been gone longer than she realized because she heard Ben calling her. She trudged through the snow back to the house.

"We better not press our luck and get out of here while we can," he told her.

Her mouth drooped down. "I suppose."

He smiled. "You like it here, don't you?"

"I do, I really do."

"Well, maybe now you will take a few days off and come up here. You are more than welcome."

"I just might do that." She had said many times she might take time off but this time she meant it.

Chapter Fourteen

The drive home was substantially less difficult.
The lull in the snowstorm gave the plow crews a chance
to catch up, although it was still slippery. They were
forced to drive well beneath the speed limit. When they
arrived home, Brian's car was in the driveway. Ben
drove into the garage where they unloaded the bags of
garbage for trash pick up and carried their things inside.
Brian was sitting at the kitchen counter picking at an
assortment of bowls of food he pilfered from the
refrigerator. He looked at their bags and said in a
lascivious tone, "Well, well, well. What have you two
been up to?"

Nora found it amusing while Ben found his
comment offensive; not that he was unused to Brian's
ribbings. He was offended for Nora. She grinned at him
while picking up her bag to take to her room.

"Nothing, you jerk," Ben snapped.

Brian stuffed more food in his mouth and nearly
choked trying not to laugh. "I don't know. You come in
here after being gone all night. I didn't think you had it
in you. What would your mother say?"

"The State Police called to tell me the cabin was
burglarized. Nora agreed to go with me to take care of
things."

Brian's fork clanged to the countertop. "That's my
getaway spot. How bad is it?"

"They trashed everything they could break but didn't take anything. I wished it were the other way around. We worked all day and into the night, but it's presentable now. I will have to replace a lot of things. It's my fault for not being more diligent about securing the place. It's empty for too long." Ben changed the subject. "So, where were you? I called you three times. I wanted you to go with me. I thought it was unfair to accept Nora's help."

He bent his head and mumbled, "I went skiing with a friend."

Ben was used to his friend's tete-a-tetes. "By the looks of your appetite, I venture the slopes weren't the only thing you hit."

"Let's not be vulgar. What about you and Nora?"

"We drove up there, worked ourselves to death, and came home. You know better than to think otherwise."

Brian slugged down a beer with his food. "I do, but it's fun to ask anyway. You are too damn honorable for your own good. I'd never let a woman like Nora escape my charms; but that's just me."

Ben shook his head and snorted at his friend. "Don't you have some place to be?"

After Brian left, Ben went into his library and pulled a notepad from his desk drawer. He kept on top of things, and it bothered him about all the items destroyed at the cabin. He wanted to replace them to ensure it was available for use to anyone who wanted a break. Even if he avoided using it, he still wanted it accessible to anyone who might need to get away. By the time he added everything up, after his deductible it wasn't worth turning it into his insurance company. As he was going over his list, he saw Nora standing over him. She was pale and wringing her hands.

"Mr. Stafford, may I take the rest of the day off; maybe even tomorrow?" She spoke so softly he strained to hear her.

"Of course, but may I ask you what's wrong?"

Her nose turned red, and she began to sniffle. "I just got a call from the hospital. They said my boyfriend is dying and wants to see me. They don't think he has much time left. I need to be there for him. I don't think he has anyone else."

He knew she referred to the World War II veteran she had befriended. He looked out the window and saw the relentless snowstorm had returned. "I better drive you."

She shook her head. "No, I cannot ask you to do that. It isn't far and it's all main roads. I have driven in worse."

He slid his chair back and stood. "Don't be ridiculous; your car is too light for this weather. Do not argue with me because I'm taking you whether you like it or not."

"I'm in no position to argue. I need to get there as soon as possible. Thank you, I appreciate it."

It was a Sunday afternoon when typically the streets were quiet, but the snowstorm left them deserted. Getting to the hospital was quicker than expected even with the pounding snow. Ben pulled up to the front door allowing Nora faster access to the elderly man's room. "I'll park the car and join you."

"That's not necessary. I don't know how long I'll be here. I will get home somehow. I do not want to inconvenience you further."

As much as he hated any hospital, Ben felt compelled to stay. "Nonsense, I owe him this last gesture of respect for everything he has done in his lifetime. What's his name so I can find his room?"

"Vincent, Vincent Pirelli," she said as she closed the car door.

It took Ben another fifteen minutes to park in the garage, walk to the hospital, and find Vincent's room. He stood in the doorway where a thin, frail old man was smiling affectionately at Nora as she held his hand. He was not connected to any machines except a heart monitor which continually beeped, breaking any moment of silence. The old man said to Nora, "I always knew you weren't really my girl, but thank you for pretending."

Nora smiled while squeezing his hand. "That's where you're wrong, Vincent. I am your girl."

With those last words the heart monitor no longer beeped, it made a long, sad tone. Nora never reacted, she simply continued to hold his hand as her lips moved in prayer. A nurse pushed by Ben, looked down at Vincent, and turned off the monitor. She said to Nora, "Stay as long as you like." Nora nodded and continued to hold his hand and stare at his lifeless face.

Ben stepped into the room and placed his hands on her shoulders. They heaved as she said, "He lived a long life and from what little he told me, it was a happy one. I wish there was more I may have done for him." She removed her hand from his grasp and placed it across his heart.

Ben never met the man, but he was not as stoic. He left the room to keep from breaking down. When the nurse turned his monitor off, it was more than he was able to endure. He lived that scene before and prayed it never happened again. He admired Nora's devotion to someone she hardly knew. To stay by his side in his last moments was more a tribute to her than to Vincent. Ben did not have her fortitude.

Nora continued to sit with Vincent for another ten minutes. She finally appeared in the hallway to join Ben. He put his arm around her shoulder to escort her down the corridor when the hospital administrator approached. "Miss Manning?"

She nodded.

"Mr. Pirelli named you as next of kin of record."

"Me?" Her head shot upward. "I barely knew him."

He smiled and spoke in a reverent tone. "It was purely a gesture of respect and affection for you. He has been a ward of the Veteran's Administration for the last ten years. There are no immediate family left and he made his final arrangements years ago to be buried next to his wife. There is nothing for which you are responsible except attend his funeral—if you so desire."

Her eyes glistened as she lovingly glanced back into Vincent's room. "Oh, of course, I'd consider it an honor."

"We'll let you know when and where. He wanted a simple graveside service. The local VFW post where he was a member will provide pallbearers with a ceremonial soldier's salute."

Ben was now composed, and it was Nora who appeared shaky. He put his arm around her waist and said in a hushed tone, "Let's go home." During the drive little was said until Ben finally broke the silence. "It's sad he has no family to mourn him."

Nora stared through the car windshield and blurted

out, "I know the feeling."

Ben turned his head toward her, but she looked straight ahead expressionless. There was a deep sadness in her eyes, but no tears. He came close to pulling the car to the side of the road with the intention to comfort her, but he did not. He felt an overwhelming urge to protect her; he just didn't know from what. The wall they both put up against life and its heartache was not as strong as they thought.

The following morning Nora received a call from the hospital administrator, informing her arrangements were made for Vincent's burial next to his wife. It was an old historic cemetery five miles outside of town. Ben was familiar with it because it was where his father and other family members were buried. "I would consider it a privilege to accompany you," Ben said.

"Thank you, the more people to honor him the better. Vincent deserves to be mourned."

At eleven the next morning Vincent's funeral began despite the blustery winds and accumulating snow. Everyone met at his gravesite bundled up against the elements, but not a single complaint was uttered. The mourners consisted of members of the VFW post, the chaplain from the hospital, and the administrator. Just as the chaplain was about to begin, a military vehicle approached. It was clear from its detailing it belonged to a general. He and two aides approached the coffin when the general interrupted the service. "I am terribly sorry we are late, but it was a long drive, and the roads are less than ideal. It is a poor excuse for a military man; you have my apologies."

Nora stared at him as the chaplain performed the simple but touching service. When he was finished, the administrator handed the general a box and pointed to Nora. It was not usual protocol, but military tradition was suspended in favor of Vincent's desire for simplicity. He stepped forward to present her with the box, then stopped abruptly in his tracks when he looked into her eyes. Ben watched the exchange of looks between the general and Nora; they knew each other despite no acknowledgement.

Without missing a beat, the general said, "Nora," then in a hesitant voice asked, "Manning?"

She stood erect and lifted her chin replying in a formal tone, "Yes, sir."

"It was Mr. Pirelli's last request you become the caretaker of this, and it is my great privilege to present it to you. It has been vigilantly and honorably safeguarded by the Veteran's Hospital."

She opened it and her hands began to shake so severely Ben moved closer to steady her. Inside was the Congressional Medal of Honor. She nearly dropped it. Ben placed his hands around hers to hold the box steady. Nora stammered, "I had no idea."

"The medal was awarded to him decades ago, but he was very private about it. He never attended any ceremonies for the honorees. Only the hospital administration knew, but I felt an obligation to give Mr. Pirelli a proper send off."

The twenty-one-gun salute was sounded, and after the flag was folded by the honor guard, the general handed it to her. There was no emotion showing on her face when she accepted it. She bowed her head as she clutched the flag to her chest to protect it from the falling snow.

The gathering dispersed to their cars to warm up

and leave; only the general, Ben, and Nora stood before the open grave. After a moment of silence, the general stepped toward Nora and said, "When they asked me to present his medal, I had no idea it was to you. Would you do me the honor of joining me for lunch?" He looked over at Ben. "Of course, Mr. Manning is welcome."

Ben stood mute. He looked from the general to Nora hoping for clarity. There was none. Nora gestured toward Ben. "This is Mr. Stafford, my employer. We must respectfully decline. On Vincent's behalf I thank you for your attendance." She politely extended her hand; the general took it pausing in his grasp. She pulled it back and headed for the car with Ben following behind her. During the drive home he thought she might answer the questions on his mind, but she did not. He finally broke their awkward silence. "I wish the chaplain or general had told us why he was awarded the Medal of Honor. That is a monumental achievement. I wonder what branch of the service he was in."

Nora had opened the box and examined it. "The army."

"Did he tell you that?"

"No, but the insignia on the medal is for the army. Each branch has its own."

He thought she knew a lot about it. When they returned home, Nora disappeared to her room while Ben went to his computer to look up Vincent's name. The internet was a wealth of information especially relating to World War II. It was not difficult to find what he was looking for and he was humbled by the man's courage under fire. He, singlehanded, saved his entire unit from certain death. He drew enemy fire upon himself to bide time for the back-up troops to arrive. He wanted to read about it all night. He was thankful he attended Vincent's funeral, but it still did not answer why Nora knew the general.

He began to wonder if she served in the military. If she served, it explained many things about her conduct and behavior. Her military knowledge, dedication to the Veteran's Hospital, and need for privacy. Possibly the long scar down her stomach was a battle wound. If she knew the horrors of war, it certainly explained her reclusive behavior. Her need for privacy and a quiet environment were all consistent with someone recovering from battle. He was almost certain it was the case, because she was so fastidious about detail and formal in demeanor. They were the habits characteristic of military discipline. Nevertheless, it still seemed unlikely a general recognized her. They were not likely to travel in the same circle. It might, however, not prevent her from knowing him. Ben had more questions than answers; he was not confident he'd ever learn the truth.

****

Upon returning home Nora immediately retreated to her room. She propped Vincent's flag up against the wall on her dresser and placed the box containing his medal next to it. She opened it again. It had aged with time. The medal was no longer brilliant, and dulled from all the years since it was first presented to Vincent. The blue ribbon to which it was attached also faded. Her fingers trembled as she ran them over it. She knew too well the sacrifice that went into him earning it. It was the only material object he owned at the end of his life; she was feeling honored beyond words he wanted her to have it. She bent down and opened her bottom dresser drawer, pulling aside articles of clothing, and produced another box. She placed it next to Vincent's and opened it. It too held a Congressional Medal of Honor, only this one still had its bright sheen, and the blue ribbon was fresh and pristine. It was not locked away for decades like Vincent's medal. She looked at each of them side by side, the same yet different. Their commonality was bravery and war, and she knew both would continue to exist until the end of time. The sacrifices each medal represented cannot be even remotely conveyed by a piece of metal dangling from a ribbon. She ran her finger across the medal and then returned the second box to its place beneath her clothing at the back of her dresser drawer.

Nora resumed business as usual, preparing dinner. She was a woman on a mission to put the day's events behind her. The familiarity of the kitchen and the task of preparing food soothed her. Ben sought her in the kitchen, reaching out to touch her arm to gain her attention. "Nora," he said in a soft voice. "Please just take a little time off. You don't have to do this."

She looked him in the eye with a determined countenance. "Yes, I do."

He lightly placed his hand on her shoulder. "If you ever have the need to talk, I'll listen."

She never doubted his sincerity, but there are wounds too deep to heal. Nevertheless, she was grateful he offered to help. "Thank you, sir, but I'm fine." She was anything but fine.

Chapter Fifteen

February was typically the coldest month of the year and this one proved to be no exception. It was ideal for people who loved winter sports, especially skiing. Ben noted that Brian was *skiing* nearly every weekend and he rarely stopped by the house. Even Nora commented on it. "The refrigerator hasn't been raided in weeks; where's Mr. McNair?"

Ben laughed at her reference. "I suspect he has a new girlfriend, and for whatever reason, he's been very tightlipped. You know that is out of character for him. Brian can keep legal confidences better than any lawyer I have ever met, but when it comes to affairs of heart; that's another story."

Ben secretly thought Brian had feelings for Nora and was staying away because he knew Ben did not approve of his lack of morals. Their friendship transcended personal values; it was unconditional. He was inclined to rethink his assessment of Brian's absence when he stopped by his office.

"Ben, is it all right if I use the cabin this weekend?"

He shrugged. "I guess so, but I haven't replaced the things which were destroyed. If you do not mind hauling them up there, I'll have Nora buy the replacements."

"Not a problem and I'll stock your liquor cabinet

too."

Ben grinned. "I don't have a liquor cabinet in the cabin."

Brian winked. "You will. I would like to use the place more often."

Ben comically banged his head on the desk. "Oh no, Brian, please don't tell me your clandestine affair is with a married woman."

"No, no, she's divorced but let us just say there are people who don't want to see us together."

Ben didn't know what he meant, but given his knowledge of Brian, it probably was not good. If there was a woman, he did not want to brag about there was a backstory. He was fearful to learn her identity. "My cabin is your cabin, but if an angry ex-husband is out for revenge, I don't want to know about it."

"I can give you my personal assurance that isn't the case." He winked at Ben. "Don't you think I've learned a thing or two over the years."

Ben grinned. "I'd trust you to manage my most complicated legal business, but your education on affairs of the heart leaves much to be desired."

Brian patted him on the back. "Not this time, buddy."

Brian had no sooner left than Ben's secretary told him there was a gentleman from the Margaret Weinstein Foundation to see him. The Weinstein Foundation was an organization which funded medical research at the local research hospital. It was the pet charity of Ben's firm and he contributed generously to it. "Send him in." A man stepped into his office; Ben got to his feet and shook his hand. "Good to you again, Harold. Please sit down."

Harold Banks made himself comfortable in a chair. "I'll get to the point; next week is our annual Valentine's Day Foundation dinner and awards ceremony."

Ben nodded. "I know. I bought my usual two tickets." He never attended the lavish dinner, instead giving the tickets to his secretary. It was an elegant evening and she worked tirelessly with the firm's fund-raising efforts.

"We need more than your money; you're this year's honoree."

Ben stared at him. There were other devoted donors who worked equally as hard at raising funds as his firm. It was no secret he never attended any of the affairs. "That's very kind of you but I don't deserve it."

"Deserve it?" Harold's voice changed to a higher pitch. "In the last year, your firm alone has raised almost two hundred thousand dollars."

"I had no idea it was that much, but nevertheless there are others more deserving than I."

Harold stood, leaned over Ben's desk, and said, "I knew you'd argue with me. You're it and that's that. Get dressed up, bring a date, and let us honor you."

There was no way out of it; he was pressured to agree. The foundation had generously contributed to the hospital, and he had been a dedicated sponsor. He reluctantly accepted.

The same evening as Nora served dinner, Ben asked, "Did you have any plans for Valentine's Day?"

Her brow furrowed and her lips formed a cockeyed smile. "Yeah, right."

He smiled because they both were aware each would be spending the night alone. "I have a huge favor to ask. I previously told you my firm contributes to a charity; well, they are giving me an award for fundraising. I cannot get out of going. I need an escort, if for no other reason than to buffer me from the whole thing. It's black tie at the Cosmopolitan Room. I am certain you heard of it."

"Thank you for the invitation, but I really cannot accept. I am hardly the type of person you'd want on your arm for a formal event."

He tried to give her his most pathetic look. "Please? I really can't go alone. If they pair me up with someone, I would probably have to engage in small talk and false interest."

She snorted. "Gee, with such an attractive invitation how can I refuse?"

His head bobbed and he covered a smile with his hand. "I'm sorry, I didn't mean to make it sound so tacky. Honestly, I consider myself privileged to have you attend with me. You know what I'm like, and I can be myself and vice-a-versa."

She threw her head back and laughed. "I knew what you meant, but confidentially, I have nothing in my wardrobe to wear to a place of the Cosmopolitan Room's caliber. I don't suppose my apron is appropriate?"

"I'll buy you the prettiest dress in town and you can finally use that spa gift certificate I gave you."

"Are you trying to tell me something?"

He grinned. "Boy, you are making this hard for me."

"I'm just joking; I can afford to buy my own dress. I have a very generous boss."

He leaned in toward her. "Then you'll go?"

****

She nodded. Her heart wasn't in it, but not because she felt inferior to anyone. She had attended similar functions in her lifetime for one reason or another. She was now a simpler person with no grand aspirations. She did appreciate his predicament; no one likes to attend such events alone, particularly when it is being held in their honor.

Nora went shopping for a gown and made an appointment at the spa. She indulged in a day of pampering, and the last thing they did was her hair. The stylist swept it up and adorned it with sequin and pearl hair pins; they even applied her makeup. If she randomly walked past a mirror, she doubted she'd recognized herself.

She went home and dressed for the banquet. Ben rapped on her door to ask if she was ready. When she opened her door, he appeared dumbstruck. She was drop dead gorgeous in a black sequined gown. She found herself feeling self conscious when stepping into the hallway.

"Wow," he said with his eyes glued on her.

"You approve?" she asked, making a quick twirl.

He stammered, "Ahh, yeah."

She made a comical curtesy to him. "You realize of course, I will never have a reason to wear this gown again."

There was appreciation in his eyes. "I'll find a reason."

"May I return the compliment. I have never seen you in a tuxedo. It suits you, no pun intended."

"I think we might be the best dressed couple in attendance," he said offering his arm to escort her to his car.

When they entered the Cosmopolitan Room, they were surrounded by Weinstein board members congratulating him on his upcoming award. He continually introduced Nora to everyone, becoming awkward when someone asked how they met. Ben stammered for an answer when Nora effortlessly replied, "We're neighbors."

When they were alone, he said, "Good answer. I wish I could think that fast."

"It's really no one's business, and it is true."

Despite his reservations about attending, Ben was having a wonderful time. He conversed with attendees, and Nora's poise and grace made everything seamlessly flow. She had a rare ability to instill a sense of calm when in her presence. They were escorted to the dais to have their dinner, listen to speeches, and await his award. He was not the only one receiving recognition; there were others who worked tirelessly for the foundation. His award was to be presented last. The award presentation was received with an unexpected result. The granddaughter of the Weinstein founder stepped to the microphone. She smiled at Ben. "We are here this evening to honor an extraordinary man, who has extended all his resources to further our cause. The cause is the diagnosis and treatment for children suffering from Leukemia."

Nora was smiling and listening to the introduction when she noticed a change in Ben. He began to wiggle in his chair and perspiration formed on his forehead.

"The funds he helped us raise will go toward revolutionary treatment of the disease and aid families who may not have the resources for advance treatment.

No one feels the pain and anguish this horrendous disease brings to the children and their families more than Benjamin Stafford. Currently, I would like to unveil this plaque. It will hang at the entrance of the new leukemia wing of the Children's Hospital." She pulled off a cover which was hanging over an easel revealing a bronze plate—*The Elizabeth Stafford Center For The Diagnosis And Treatment Of Leukemia.*

Nora quickly turned to Ben. She correctly surmised he lost a daughter, but the circumstances were previously unknown to her. He was white, his hands were shaking, and he looked like he was about to vomit. He stood up so quickly his chair tipped over as he fled from the room. There was a deafening silence. No one knew what to say or do. Nora did not know what came over her when she stood and went to the microphone. She looked out at the audience as they remained awkwardly silent.

"As you can see Mr. Stafford was overwhelmed by this unexpected honor. On his behalf I would like to accept this award in the memory of his beloved daughter Elizabeth. Thank you."

There was thunderous applause, then she too left the dais in search of him. She found him standing outside in the freezing parking lot seemingly oblivious to the cold. He was openly weeping. "How could they do this to me?" he asked her with such heart-wrenching despair she wanted to cry with him.

She searched for words; she did not want to say anything to make him feel worse. "They didn't think they were doing it to you; they were doing it for you. I cannot tell you how to handle this; I've never lost a child. What I do know for certain, there isn't a worse experience or a deeper loss. I also believe this cause is important to you. The well-intentioned but poorly executed manner in which they gave you a well-deserved tribute is secondary to your feelings. So many children will benefit from your tragedy and efforts to make Elizabeth's death stand for something. Tonight, you proved her death did matter; it mattered to every person in that room. It will matter to every child you help save."

Tears streamed down his face. "Do you think I'm being selfish?"

She wiped his tears with her bare hand and said in a gentle voice, "Absolutely not. No one has the right to assign emotions to another, especially under these circumstances. We all grieve and love in our own way. When, how, or if you decide to heal is not for anyone else to say."

Ben lifted his head to stare at the door he had just fled. "I suppose I have to go back in there and say something."

"I took care of it. I accepted on your behalf."

"You?" His voice cracked. "You are the shyest person I know."

"It was for a worthy cause. Let's get our coats and go home."

He took her arm. "I don't know how to thank you. I wouldn't have survived this without you."

She tried to lighten the mood. "Next time I'll wear my superhero cape."

****

Once back at the house, Nora headed for her room when Ben called after her. "Can I offer you a brandy with me in the living room? I don't want to drink alone."

"All right," she said following behind him.

They sat in large comfortable chairs opposite one another, which was more conducive for having a conversation. Ben poured the amber liquid into two crystal brandy snifters. He swallowed his brandy in just two sips and poured another as the warmth of it took its hold. Nora never lifted the snifter to her lips.

"Now you know what I've tried not to think about."

"I already knew."

He set his snifter down and looked at her. "How? Everyone has been walking on eggshells around me for the past five years. I'm certain no one talked to you about it."

She took a tiny sip of brandy before she answered. "You can't live in someone's home and not pick up on another's person's pain. I didn't know the details until tonight, but I knew you lost a daughter. I wondered when I saw the picture you were looking at from your wallet when Sarah was here. The Christmas ornament and how it affected you so deeply confirmed it, and there were other things."

With eyebrows furrowed he said, "You never said anything."

"Why would I? If you wanted me to know, you'd tell me. I'm your employee, it's not my place."

He slowly shook his head. "You're more than that. I think of you as a trusted friend. I know we haven't exactly confided in each other, but I'm certain I know who you are inside."

She bowed her head as if she were examining her shoes. "Thank you. I trust you too which has made my life here feel like I have a real sense of security."

The effects of the brandy were taking hold. He felt the need to unburden himself. "I want to tell you about Elizabeth."

"You don't have to if it's too painful. You don't owe me an explanation."

"It's time," he said taking a deep breath. "Elizabeth could have been Sarah's identical twin if they were the same age." He smiled as he continued, "She was pretty, smart, and vivacious. When she first became ill, her mother and I didn't think it was anything serious; she was only four. Children don't get sick, or at least that's what we thought. We watched her go through chemo, radiation, bone marrow transplants; every cruel ungodly thing you can imagine."

He paused as he wiped a tear from his face with the back of his hand. "She was so brave and good about it. She comforted us more than the other way around. She lingered for weeks, and we never left her side. I watched you hold Vincent's hand as he died; that's what I did with Lizzie. I was trying desperately to transfer her disease to me, so she'd be free. Isn't that ridiculous?"

He detected the same despair in Nora's face when she said, "No. I understand better than you might imagine."

"When Lizzie let go of this world so did I. I have never reconciled myself to her death."

Nora's voice was tender. "What about her mother?"

"Connie?" When he said her name aloud a smile crossed his lips. "We met in graduate school and were soon inseparable. She was Lizzie in grown up form—

beautiful, funny, kind, everything a man wants in a wife and partner for life. We grieved together, but she was eventually able to move past the pain. She wanted to remember Lizzie for the joy she brought into our lives and not the agony we endured when she left it. I just couldn't do that. Connie tried to help me. She wanted to go to counseling and support groups, but I just wanted to drink and be left alone. Eventually she gave me my wish and left. I don't have one ounce of animosity toward her, I would have done the same thing."

"What happened to her?"

Taking another sip of brandy, he replied, "She moved back to Chicago where she grew up. Brian's ex-wife keeps in touch with her. She remarried and gave birth to twin sons a couple of years ago."

"Does that bother you?"

He tilted his head back against the chair and sighed. "Yes and no. Yes, because she has moved on and I've been left behind; no, because she deserves all the happiness she can find. I have a lot of faults but I'm not vindictive; I want the best for her."

"I don't think anyone would ever accuse you of vindictiveness. As I said before, when you live in the same house with someone you learn things. What I've learned about you is, you're a kind and honorable man. You're allowed to be happy; it's not disrespectful to Elizabeth."

He took another drink from his glass. "That's the point; I can't get past the pain. How can I be happy when she is gone?"

"Do you wish her back to continue where she left off? Elizabeth was loved and protected by her parents who were powerless to help her. You lovingly and responsibly helped her transition to a better place."

Ben did not respond but he nodded in acknowledgment. He discerned the conversation was getting entirely too personal to suit Nora. She avoided eye contact and lifted her brandy snifter gulping the rest of the liquid. It made her cough. "It's late; I think I'll retire now. Thank you for allowing me to share Elizabeth's legacy."

She stood to leave, but Ben reached out to stop her. "Nora, are you leaving because you're tired or are you afraid I'll ask what you are running from?"

Her voice was breathless. "Both."

Chapter Sixteen

Monday morning found Ben back at work. He was trying to put behind him the events which took place at the awards ceremony. As he was pouring over financial spreadsheets Brian barged into his office. "Have lunch with me. There is something I want to tell you."

Ben set aside his paperwork, giving Brian his full attention. He was used to his friend being spontaneous, but his request seemed important. "All right."

They went to a small restaurant near Ben's office they often frequented. It was a favorite spot for local businesspeople to meet for lunch. Ben and Brian knew at least half a dozen people. When Brian was not distracted by stopping to speak with each of them, Ben knew something was up. "Okay, what's so urgent?"

"Hold onto your seat." He began making the sound of a drumroll. "I'm getting married." He was more excited than Ben had ever seen, and Brian had the exuberance of a kid on caffeine.

He blindsided Ben, and instead of being happy for his friend, he was worried. "Oh, Brian. You've only been dating this woman a few weeks. You cannot possibly know her well enough to get married, and frankly you're a serial cheater."

He displayed no offense. "You're wrong. I know her better than anyone else, besides you."

Ben did not want to hurt his feelings but felt

compelled to express his concerns. "I know you think that. Whenever someone is in *love,* it is what they believe, and then when it's too late they realize they were wrong. I don't want to see you make a mistake, for her sake as well as yours."

Brian giggled like a schoolboy. "You don't even know who I'm marrying."

"That's my point. You have been seeing her for a short amount of time and being secretive about it. None of our friends know her. That should tell you something right there, you've kept her from us."

"You all know her," he said leaning back in his chair.

A realization came to Ben, and he gasped. "Oh no, please tell me it is not Rick Lander's ex-wife. That's why you said there were people who wouldn't like it. You have flirted shamelessly with her for years. He's the district attorney for goodness sakes. What are you thinking?"

Brian nearly choked from laughter. "No, it's not his ex-wife; it's mine."

Ben had been taking a sip of water and spit it back in his glass before he was able to swallow it. "Molly? I'd have given you better odds with Rick's ex."

"Yes, Molly." He leaned forward toward Ben. "I've finally grown up, and I have Nora to thank for it."

He didn't think Brian was capable of surprising him further, but he was wrong. "Nora?"

"I saw all the qualities in her I missed in Molly. They are both down to earth, kind, thoughtful, and more than anything else, dependable. I watched Nora care for you when you were sick. I realized there was nothing Molly wouldn't do for me if I was in your place. I'm different, honestly. I don't want to be picking women up at bars, hiding from their phone calls and texts, and looking for my next conquest. I want a steady home, children, and a wife who screws up the checkbook."

"When did all this happen?"

"Christmas. As I sat with you and Nora, I, for the first time, realized what I missed. I love you like a brother, but I'd rather spend Christmas with a wife, dog, and maybe a kid or two. We had our first real in-depth conversation since our divorce. As you know, we've always remained friends, which helped enormously to move us beyond the past. We set boundaries and goals. She has changed too. She is no longer the quiet suffering type as she was when I was fooling around. She wouldn't tolerate it now, and I respect that. I proposed on Valentine's Day at your cabin."

Ben was trying to process the news, but he was unbelievably happy for Brian. Molly was everything he said she was just like his ex-wife Connie, but Brian had a do-over chance. Ben's chance had passed years ago. It did not stop him from being grateful Brian had the opportunity to make amends. He stood up to embrace him. "Buddy, I can't tell you how happy I am for you, not Molly, but you."

"Ha, ha," Brian said. "I won't screw it up this time, promise."

Ben was sure he meant it. The past year he saw a change in Brian. He felt it indirectly had something to do with Nora. She brought out the best in people. He wanted the same for her.

Brian's demeanor turned serious. "Ben, the same thing is right in front of you. Take a chance."

He was referring, of course, to Nora but Brian was not privileged to the things he knew. Nora may not even be available. If she were, he didn't know where to begin to approach her, or if it was even a good idea. "It's not that simple, Brian."

"Why not?"

"My past. I don't know if I'm good for anyone. I don't want to drag another person down with me."

"You won't; I think you're afraid of intimacy."

He knew there was more than a grain of truth to what Brian said, but the same may be true of Nora. He wasn't ready to screw up her life, his was already a mess.

When he returned home after work, his usual drink was waiting for him. He picked it up and went into the kitchen. He found Nora chopping vegetables in preparation for dinner.

She looked up and said, "Good afternoon, Mr. Stafford. Is there something I can get for you?"

He snatched one of the carrots she was slicing and started to munch on it. "I've got something to tell you and you won't believe it."

Her attention was back on the vegetables. "What?"

"I had lunch with Brian this afternoon; he told me he is getting married."

Nora's knife stopped in mid chop. "Married? Mr. McNair? He told me once when he was ready to grow up, he wanted to marry, but I didn't think it would be this soon. How long has he known her?"

"Funny, that was the first thing I asked him. This is where the plot thickens."

She placed her knife on the cutting and turned to give him her full attention. "Don't keep me in suspense."

"It's his ex-wife, Molly."

"I think that's heartwarming they are going to try again. Will it work this time?"

He reached for another carrot. "I think it will. I'm seeing a different side of him, and he credits you."

"Me?" she asked with surprise in her voice.

"Apparently you touched a domestic chord in him."

"I will only be flattered if they stay married. I really like him; he is sometimes a little off the wall, but he's a good person at heart."

Nodding, he replied, "He's the best. I agree with you that he can be a little flakey, but I can't tell you how important and stabilizing a person he was when I lost Lizzy. There were moments when I wasn't sure I'd make it through another day. He dropped everything for me and never left my side. He was still married to Molly at the time, and she did the same thing for Connie. Those are the acts of kindness you can never repay."

"Those are the acts of kindness you never expect to be repaid. You know one day it may be your turn to reciprocate."

"And I would." He picked up his drink and headed for his library.

****

The relentless winter weather finally broke, and spring was in the air. As the days became warmer, Ben was elated when he found the first buds in his garden. Each day he checked the shrubs and examined the trees hoping it meant spring was here to stay. He pored over the book Nora bought him for Christmas and made new plans for his yard. The new beginning spring offered seemed to affect Ben in a way it had not in prior years. Ever since he unburdened himself to Nora about his daughter, things had changed. He did not feel the same weight on his shoulders. His relationship with Nora, however, remained unchanged. They still maintained their formality, yet it too was different. There was an unspoken emotional intimacy between them, but not so intimate she allowed herself to share her heartbreak.

Brian asked Ben if he and Molly may marry in his backyard as soon as it was in full bloom. "Hey, buddy, can you do me a huge favor?"

In years past when Brian asked for a huge favor it usually meant covering for one of his trysts, however he was confident his friend had changed. "I'm almost afraid to answer." Ben smiled.

"I've spent so many days in your backyard, enjoying all the work you put into making it your own little paradise; Molly and I want to be married there."

Relieved it wasn't some absurd request, Ben said, "I'd be honored. It will give me an excuse to spruce it up with some of the ideas in the book Nora gave me."

"Spruce up? The Gardens of Versailles can't compare to yours."

Brian and Molly only had to wait three more weeks before Ben's backyard was at its spring peak. It was going to be a small affair with no more than thirty people. Nora offered, as her gift, to do all the catering. "I think Mr. McNair's garden wedding idea is brilliant. It has more meaning than a Justice of the Peace and a restaurant buffet. If you have no objections, I would like to cater the reception."

Ben thought it was an extremely generous offer,

and an ambitious one. "Are you sure? It seems like an enormous amount of work."

"I hosted larger groups at the inn with fewer amenities. I'm not worried about doing it justice."

"I am certain it won't be less than perfection. I will supply the liquor and cover the food cost as my gift to them."

****

At Brian's urging, Nora finally had the opportunity to meet Molly. They got together to go over the menu and garden arrangements. She was everything Ben said, and Nora understood why Brian wanted to reconcile with her. He was an idiot to let her go and extremely fortunate she did not marry someone else. After speaking with her it was obvious, she never stopped loving him. She told Nora she prayed for the day he became the man she always knew he was inside. Molly and Nora sat at the patio table going over the details for the reception. "I cannot tell you how grateful I am you are doing this for us. This is the kind of wedding I wanted the first time around."

Nora asked, "Why, what was wrong with the first one?"

Molly's face contorted when she answered. "It was an elaborate *dog and pony show*. We had a big church wedding with a half a dozen bridesmaids and groomsmen followed by a reception at an expensive banquet facility."

Nora shrugged. "That doesn't seem so bad."

Molly leaned in closer and almost whispered, "It does when your marriage doesn't last more than a few years. If anyone told me I would be remarrying Brian, I'd tell them they were crazy."

Nora patted her arm. "There are things which are meant to be. We all evolve from experiences in life. Some things we discard and others we embrace. You and Mr. McNair were meant to be together. You are fortunate the changes you each went through brought you back to the same place."

Molly's chest heaved as she took a deep breath. "I hope you're right. It wasn't all his fault; I should have done some things differently."

"There isn't a person on the face of the earth who hasn't thought the same thing."

"It sounds like you speak from experience."

Nora sensed a sympathetic chord in Molly's voice. For a moment she was tempted to reveal, at the very least, a small part of her pain. She stayed silent knowing it was imprudent. She found herself enjoying her company, which she feared may present a problem. If they became friends, it may cause an awkward situation if she and Brian wanted to socialize with her and Ben. She felt it was best to keep the same cordial efficiency with Molly she enjoyed with Ben and Brian.

****

The wedding was everything the couple hoped. The weather cooperated, Nora's hors d'oeuvres and entrees were well received by the guests. Most importantly Brian and Molly were blissfully happy. Her father escorted her down the garden path to Ben's gazebo where the guests had gathered. She chose a simple white dress and carried a bouquet of wildflowers. From the expression on their faces, it was difficult to discern who was happier, Molly or Brian. The guests laughed when Molly's father made a point of saying to Brian, "Don't screw it up this time." A judge Brian knew from the court performed a simple civil ceremony. It was the wedding Molly told Nora she wanted the first time around. They left after the reception for a weeklong honeymoon in the Virgin Islands.

Ben insisted Nora hire extra help to serve and clean up. As the perfectionist she was, she started to gather up dishes and glasses. He grabbed her arm when she walked by him and said firmly, "Sit and relax. Let the crew do the job they were hired to do. I saw the enormous amount of work which went into all the preparation, and you deserve a break."

She smiled as she sank into a chair. "I am tired. I think I'm a little out of practice. I used to be able to cater events like this one every other week and not even break a sweat."

"The inn's loss is my gain," he said then added, "I don't know how I got along without you."

He reached behind him and picked up a half empty bottle of champagne and two glasses. "Here," he said, pouring her a glass. "Let's drink to Molly and Brian."

They clinked glasses and sipped the champagne. Ben turned his head around to take in his garden. "It has been years since I have enjoyed the grounds like I have today. I guess when you can share it, it means more."

Nora looked around too. "Everything is better when it's shared. It makes the good better and the bad tolerable. This is a memory I will cherish. It's not often people get a second chance."

Ben chuckled. "I think every person in attendance agreed with Molly's father about telling Brian not to screw it up."

****

After a carefree week in the sun and sand, Molly and Brian returned to begin their new life. When they decided to remarry, he put his condominium up for sale and moved back home, to the delight of their dog, Barker. Brian was always cheerful, but his perpetual good spirit now annoyed Ben. Upon his return the friends met for a game of handball. "I don't remember you being this happy the first time around."

Huffing and puffing chasing after the ball, Brian replied, "I was too stupid to know what I had. It's not too late for you."

Ben pulled the towel from around his neck to wipe the sweat from his face. "I think that ship sailed years ago. Not everyone is meant for blissful matrimony."

Brian snickered. "There was a time when I thought that was an oxymoron. Did I tell you we have decided to start a family as soon as possible?"

"Don't you think you should wait a bit?" Ben asked, concerned he may be rushing into something. He wanted his friend to enjoy the honeymoon phase, even if it was the second time around.

Brian and Ben headed for the locker room before he answered. "This isn't our first rodeo and we're not getting any younger. I don't want to be the oldest father in my kids' classes."

"Better old than divorced."

Brian slammed the gym locker door so hard it startled Ben. "Why are you so pessimistic? Don't try to ruin this for me."

Ben apologized. "I'm sorry; I didn't mean to be. I think I'm just a little jealous."

"Of my marriage or because I'm not as available as I used to be?"

"Probably a little of each. Honestly, I don't begrudge you your happiness. Go for it."

"How about you and Nora joining us for dinner? Molly isn't the cook Nora is, but she's pretty damn good."

Ben opened his gym locker and pulled out his street clothes. "No, I don't think so. She may get the wrong message."

Brian placed his hand on Ben's shoulder. "No, she's apt to get the right one, but I won't push it."

It was fortunate Nora never knew about their conversation. Ben had too much respect for her to put her on the spot. Theirs was a delicate balance of employer/employee and friendship. It was only natural Brian and Molly wanted to share their newfound bliss. Ben, however, felt uncomfortable with Brian's constant attempts to unite him with Nora. He was still adjusting to having shared his personal demons with her. It wasn't easy for him to let go of the anger and angst he felt after losing Elizabeth. Nora was the first outside person he openly discussed it with, and he hoped she may one day feel the same. He was willing to wait; he lived in suspended animation for so many years he recognized it in her.

Nora, in her shy and quiet manner, gave him the confidence to let go of his past. He finally realized the only thing keeping him going was punishing himself for something beyond his control. He did not know how closely Nora identified with him on that very emotion.

Chapter Seventeen

Ben was working on a financial merger which, although going very well, was painstakingly complicated. He left for work early and stayed late, but he always kept Nora informed of his plans. She worked hard keeping the house to his schedule; he did not want her cooking a meal he did not have time to eat. When he told her he was never certain what the day would bring, she laughed. "I work for you, remember?"

He went to the office and started cursing at himself. The very file he needed for his meeting was still sitting on his desk at home. He was sure he put it in his briefcase. After he pulled everything out to no success, he called Nora. "Can you check my desk and see if I left an orange file folder on it?"

She came back to the phone a minute later. "Is it labeled Mayer?"

"Yes," he said, relieved he had not left it someplace. It was uncharacteristic of him to be absent minded, but he was frazzled by the enormity of the project. "I've got a meeting in a half hour, and I need the file. I don't have time to drive home and back. Is it possible for you to bring it to me?"

"Sure, not a problem; I'll leave right now."

He exhaled heavily into the phone receiver. "You're a lifesaver."

****

When Nora did not arrive, Ben started watching the clock. All the parties involved were gathered in the conference room and waiting for the meeting to begin. First, he called home to see if she had left, but the answering machine came on. Then he called her cell phone, but it went directly to voicemail. He was worried because there was no more responsible person alive than Nora. He explained to his clients the situation and asked them to bear with him for a few more minutes, then his cell phone rang. Thankfully, Nora's number came up on the caller ID. "Thank goodness," Ben began. "I was worried something happened."

An unfamiliar voice asked, "Mr. Stafford?"

He was not prepared for someone else to speak and stepped into the hallway to take the call. "Who is this?"

"Officer Dan Stein with the Cheswick Police Department. There has been an accident involving the owner of this phone. This was the emergency number in the directory, so I called it. Do you know a Nora Manning?"

Ben felt his heart begin to pound. "What happened? Is she okay?"

"A car ran a red light at Main and Fourth streets, it T-boned her in the driver's side. I'm afraid she is severely injured. The ambulance is taking her to the Veteran's Hospital. Are you her next of kin?"

He was so short of breath he barely uttered a response. "Is she badly hurt?"

"Next of kin is for consent purposes, I really do not know the extent of her injuries. Rescue used the Jaws of Life to cut her from the vehicle."

"I'll be right there."

Ben dashed back into the conference room and

pulled his associate Mark aside. He briefly explained what happened before he rushed to the hospital. On his way to the hospital, he passed by the accident scene and watched as Nora's car was being loaded onto a flatbed trailer. He was sickened; there was nothing left of it. He was not aware a large part of what he perceived to be from the accident was, in fact, done when *they cut her out of the* car.

He sprinted into the emergency room, frantically asking everyone he saw where he might find her. A uniformed officer stood at the nurse's desk, filling out an accident form. Ben went directly to him and recognized the name on his ID tag as the one who called him. "Is she alive?" Ben demanded. "Why is she here? Why isn't she at the trauma hospital? It's no further away."

"When I checked her purse for identification, I saw her medical insurance was with the Veteran's Hospital," Officer Stein said. "We had to send her here."

Ben's mind raced in a million different directions. If her insurance was through the VA, then he was right to believe she served in the military. He stopped the first nurse he saw. "Can I see Nora Manning?"

"Not just yet. Are you family?"

Knowing she had no parents or siblings he said, "Yes."

The nurse, who was exceedingly kind and undoubtedly experienced in dealing with distressed loved ones, said, "When she is stabilized the doctor will come to speak with you."

The only thing Ben thought to do was call Brian who dropped everything and rushed to the hospital.

When Brian arrived, Ben nearly lost what little emotional reserve he had. He knew it was safe to place part of his burden on his friend.

Brian asked the same question as Ben had, "Why is she here?"

Unfortunately, the VA hospitals of the past did not have the best reputation, but the post-Vietnam and current wars forced them into the twenty-first century. They now were equipped with ultramodern medical equipment. Ben explained the insurance coverage.

"Why does she have VA coverage?"

His question became increasingly convoluted. A nurse was trying to piece together a medical history for Nora's file. When she discovered no one had pertinent answers to her questions, she became concerned. "Where are her relatives?"

Neither Ben nor Brian had answers. With no one to speak for this amazing woman, Ben felt himself dying inside because he felt totally helpless. The doctor spoke with him and Brian. The only reason they were given any information at all was because Brian claimed to be Nora's attorney.

"The good news is the only broken bones are her ribs. We're grateful they didn't puncture her lungs. She sustained numerous lacerations. There are more sutures and staples in her than I care to count. The real concern is her head injury. She has not regained consciousness and it is a waiting game for right now. We did an EEG and have not detected any major abnormalities, but time will be the only real indicator. Do you know who has her health care proxy?"

Ben looked on helplessly as Brian said, "As her attorney, I do. I will bring it by as soon as possible."

After the doctor left, Ben asked, "How do you propose to do that? We don't know anything about her family."

"I'll go see Judge King and explain the situation. From what Nora has told both of us, which is truly little, I don't think she has anyone to speak for her. A guardian must be appointed one way or another so it might as well be me. I'm not doing anything illegal or unethical, I'm just hastening the procedure, which is exactly what we need right now."

Ben agreed, but he also did not tell him he knew she had in-laws. She had never spoke of them again and he wanted to respect her privacy. While Brian did his best to get official legal standing, Ben needed to see her. He had to see for himself that she was alive. A nurse came in and told him she was being moved to the intensive care unit and once she was settled, he would be allowed to see her. It seemed like an eternity, but he only waited another forty-five minutes. When he was told it was all right to go in, he was heartbroken. She was hardly recognizable between the bruising and swelling of her face. If he had randomly walked into the room, he would not even have known it was her. He sat down next to her taking her hand in his. It was cold and unresponsive. He prayed for Brian to make a quick return.

****

It was seven o'clock in the evening before Brian reappeared. He had two things with him—a limited medical power of attorney and full knowledge of everything there was to know about Nora Manning Bauer. The first he shared with Ben and the hospital; the second would remain his secret until he spoke directly with Nora. "How is she doing?"

"The same," Ben said. "She's still unconscious."

"I'd like to see her. I am technically responsible for her care."

Ben escorted Brian into her room. "I've got to warn you, it's not pretty."

It was an understatement. Brian was not prepared for what he saw. He was sickened by the pathetic sight before him. "Good God!" he exclaimed.

"The doctor said she looks worse than she is, excepting of course, for the head injury. It's largely wait and see at this moment. Did the judge give you a tough time?" Ben asked.

"No, not really. Once I was able to provide information she had no immediate relatives and was willing to accept responsibility for her proper care, he was fine with it. It is not a complete power of attorney; it's restricted, specifically to this situation."

Ben resumed his vigil by her bedside. "As long as she is getting good care, that's all I am concerned about. I am not happy she wasn't sent to the trauma hospital. The staff assured me with all the war veterans they are treating now, she is being well cared for."

"If you want to get cleaned up and something to eat, I'll stay with her," Brian offered.

Ben clung to her hand and fixated on her. "No, at least not yet. I'd like to wait until she wakes up."

"It might be a while, and you're not much good to her if you're exhausted."

Never taking his eyes off her he replied, "I'll wait. You know I've been in this position before."

A nurse approached Brian and said, "The medical director asked to see you. He received the papers from the court and wants to discuss it with you."

Reluctantly Brian left Ben and Nora for the medical director's office. "Is everything in order to your satisfaction?"

He motioned for Brian to take a seat. "Yes, it's fine and her insurance is in order, but the last name is different."

"Yes, I know. She chose to return to her family name," Brian said, giving the impression he knew all about her.

"That's not a problem. It is not uncommon for women use their own last names. She was in the data bank, but that's not the reason I wanted to speak with you. We need to be able to contact you if things change. I wanted to make sure we have all your contact information correct. The doctor said there is another man with her. I assume he is not her husband?"

"That is her employer and close friend. I am afraid he is feeling guilty about the accident because she was running an errand for him at the time." Brian cleared his throat and hesitantly continued, "I presume from the files at the VA you know about her husband."

He shook his head. "Yes, not the whole story, but enough."

"I'd appreciate it if nothing was said to her employer about her personal life."

The administrator bristled and his tone was indignant. "Mr. McNair, we do not make it a practice to talk about our patients to anyone unauthorized to hear it."

Brian apologized. "Please forgive me, it was an inappropriate remark. He will be helping to care for her during her convalescence. Her current treatment is of immense importance to him, and as her representative, you have my permission to speak with him about it. It is her past medical treatment I think she would like to keep private until she is able to discuss it herself."

"Understood, but it is not something which will appear on her current file, although the attending physicians need to know. I will speak with them."

Brian went back to the intensive care unit where Ben was still with Nora. "Ben, you cannot stay here. They have limited hours."

He was defiant in his response. "I'll go into the ICU waiting area, but I'm not leaving."

Brian knew it was pointless to argue. "Okay, but call me if you need me and make sure you get something to eat. I will at least bring you a change of clothing in the morning."

****

It was one of the longest nights Ben ever spent and he had a great deal of experience at it. Every opportunity he got, he sat in a chair next to her bed, stared into her bruised face, praying she would open her eyes. He tried to will it to happen, just as he tried to will away Elizabeth's leukemia. He was afraid of losing her now when he felt so close to opening his heart again.

****

Brian was not feeling any better except he now had Molly. He was so exhausted, he practically dragged himself through the front door. Naturally, he told Molly what happened, but he did not share what he knew about Nora's past. Molly made Brian a drink and sat next to him on the sofa rubbing his neck. "How is Nora?"

He downed half the drink before he replied, "She is at least stable, which is more than I can say for Ben. He won't go home."

"Do you think either of them realize how much they love each other?" Molly asked.

He leaned his head into his wife's chest with love and complete exhaustion "Not consciously, but it's coming; I hope."

Molly's voice cracked. "Is she going to make it?"

"My gut tells me this woman is a survivor, and if anyone can make it, it's Nora." He stroked his wife's cheek. "Have I told you how much I love you and how blessed I am we got another chance?"

She smiled. "I feel it every day. God never gives with both hands; sometimes we must learn the hard way."

He snorted a weak laugh. "Sometimes I need a tutor."

"Do you think I should go to the hospital?" Molly asked.

"Probably, but not until she wakes up. She is going to need your help when she comes home."

"You went to such lengths to be appointed her guardian; is there no one else? No one who should come here?"

"No one I found. She is very much alone, probably because she wants it that way," he said careful not to reveal anything of a confidential matter.

"I can't help Ben?"

Brian shook his head. "Nothing can help him until she comes to, and he can speak with her for himself."

****

Ben settled himself in for the night in the ICU

184

waiting room. At midnight, a sympathetic nurse dragged a recliner chair into Nora's unit. She let him sleep there until they needed to attend to her. He hunkered down in the chair. "Thank you. I need to be here."

The nurse smiled. "We'll kick you out if it becomes necessary."

When Elizabeth was dying, Ben was always afraid to leave her because he felt his presence was keeping her alive. With Nora, he was afraid to leave because he believed she was keeping *him* alive.

As he reclined in the chair, he reached over and fell asleep holding her hand. He did not wake until the nurse gently nudged to say they needed to change her bandages and perform diagnostic tests. He looked over at Nora and felt his heart skip a few beats. If it was possible, she looked worse and, in his panic, he said as much to the nurse.

She gave him a reassuring smile. "Take a good look at her, Mr. Stafford. The swelling in her face is down. The bruises look worse because as they take their course, they look bad before they look better. Take heart; her vitals are strong, and we have every reason to believe she will recover."

He was not sure if she was placating him or telling him the truth. He did know bruises looked worse a day after an injury. The nurse seemed so calm and professional he was inclined to believe her.

An hour later Brian appeared with a change of clothes, a toothbrush, razor, and comb. "You look awful."

"My looks are the least of my worries."

"The nurses said she had an uneventful night."

Ben frowned. "Uneventful? That's the best information they gave you?"

Brian gave Ben's shoulder a squeeze. "Uneventful is good at this point. They are awaiting the results of new brain scans. I have permission for you to use the staff shower area. Go clean up. If Nora sees you this way, she will think she's worse than she is. No point in scaring her."

Ben took the bag of toiletries from Brian but paused long enough to seek reassurance. "You'll stay with her?"

Brian replied without hesitation, "Of course, I will."

****

After they finished the tests, the nurse allowed Brian to go inside Nora's room. A physician came into the room and recognized Brian as her legal representative. "She has been through a horrible trauma, and as long as we are not able to detect any blood clots in her brain, we expect her to regain consciousness any time. If she is too agitated, we may have to put her in a medically induced coma. I would prefer to wait and see what happens."

"I would think you'd want her conscious to speak with her."

"Her fractured ribs are potentially dangerous if they puncture her lungs. She must remain immobile for a while to give them a chance to start healing. You'd be surprised how quickly it happens."

The doctor gave him a light slap on the back and told him to be patient. The only thing Brian thought was *thank God the doctor did not say that to Ben. He'd have decked the guy.*

****

When Ben came back, he looked much better. A shower and fresh clothing made him feel more human, but now he was hungry. A vending machine in the ICU waiting room offered sandwiches. After one taste, he grimaced, and then laughed out loud. Nora would be appalled if she knew he was eating something this bad.

Brian came into the waiting room. "You can go back in and sit with her if you want. I will be in my office. Is there anything I need to do or get for you?"

Ben shook his head. "I called the office. Mark will wrap up the merger. He is more than capable."

"Okay then, I'll be back later."

Ben resumed his vigil, and an aide brought him a newspaper to help pass the time. He read the national and international headlines. When he turned to the local section, he was distressed to see a picture of Nora's demolished car and a police description of the accident. They never mentioned her name, pending notification of her family. He further read the other driver was a teenager who had been texting when he ran the red light; he did not require treatment. He looked over at poor Nora and thought if he had that kid in front of him, he would wring his neck.

Later that afternoon as Ben found himself dozing in the chair, still holding her hand, he jolted awake when her fingers moved beneath his. Nora stared at him looking scared and confused. So relieved to see her awake, he said, "You'll be fine. I'm just going to ring for the nurse."

The unit nurse hurried in. She took one look at Nora and smiled. "How are you feeling?"

Nora tried to speak but nothing came out. Ben saw

the distressed look in her eyes as she glanced from the nurse to him. He did not know what to say, but the nurse clearly did. "Don't be concerned, Nora. You have been unconscious, poked, prodded, and medicated. Give it a couple of hours. I will let the doctor know you're awake."

When Nora looked at Ben, the helplessness in her eyes nearly broke his heart. He wondered if she knew how seriously she was hurt. While they waited for the doctor he asked, "Do you remember anything?"

She shook her head. He explained. "You were in a car accident while you were bringing a file to my office," he said. "You are in the Veterans' Hospital. The only thing the doctors are worried about is your head injury. Now that you are awake, you'll be fine, I just know it."

He tried to sound optimistic, but he was still very worried. He watched her touch her hand to her head to feel the bandages and the spot where her hair had been shaved. "It's just hair, it'll grow back."

She started to look closely at her arms. It was the only body part visible. She ran her finger over the sutures then fell back to sleep. Relieved that she didn't ask for a mirror, he hoped she had a chance to heal a bit more before she saw the extent of her injuries.

****

Brian stopped by on his way home from the office and found Nora during one of her waking moments. She managed a smile and vocalized a weak, "Hi."

Despite his distress for her overall condition, he used his usual chipper tone. "You gave us quite a scare. I was afraid you wouldn't be able to cook dinner Saturday."

She smiled again and fell asleep. He looked at Ben. "I think it's safe for you to leave now. You have got to get some rest."

"I slept here."

Brian didn't let up. "I mean in a real bed with sheets and pillows and blankets."

A nurse happened to walk in at that moment. "Mr. Stafford, the danger is past. Right now, she is facing an extended recovery process, but she will recover."

Acting as backup for the nurse, Brian said, "I had an extensive conversation with her doctors, and they said the same thing. She will be out of the hospital in as little as a week if everything goes as expected."

Ben glanced at him. "Then what?"

"Then we can have a conversation about her care. I know you will want to take her back home and hire nurses to care for her. It is the best place for her."

Ben nodded. "Of course, I'll do anything."

Chapter Eighteen

Nora's recovery progressed at a steady pace but not quick enough to suit her. She felt guilty because every time she awoke, Ben was there at her bedside. Finally, she found the strength to say, "Mr. Stafford, you can't spend so much time here."

He gave her a half-hearted smile. "Why, are you sick of me?"

She laughed but wished she hadn't because of the pain in her ribcage. It made her short of breath as she answered, "It's very kind of you to spend so much time with me." She swallowed hard to clear her throat. "But you have an important merger."

His face contorted into a grimace. "The merger is what put you here. I will never forgive myself for your accident."

She tried to speak again but the pain limited her ability to talk. She touched his arm so he would look directly at her. "Don't be ridiculous," she squeaked out. "You said some kid was texting." She began to cough and held her sides to minimize painful movement before continuing. "You can't hold yourself responsible. It could have happened to anyone."

"But it didn't. It happened because I let myself get absorbed in my work to the point it was all I thought about. I was careless and forgot the file. I wish there was a way to take back my phone call to you."

She fumbled for the button to adjust her bed. If she sat upright, she thought it would give him the impression she wasn't in so much pain. The look of despair on his face and his disheveled appearance concerned her. He was always meticulously put together in his dress and manner. This was not the man she knew. She attempted to minimize his guilt. "If the situation were reversed, I'd not blame myself."

"Yes, you would. You are always thinking of others. You volunteer here at the veteran's wing of the hospital. You planned a Halloween party for my niece and single-handedly catered Brian and Molly's reception." He leaned over her and added, "Not to mention everything you do for me."

A tear dripped from her eyes. "That's my job."

"It's more than that, it's your calling and I feel like I take advantage of you."

She tried, unsuccessfully, to lean toward him, gave up and collapsed back on the pillows. "Then we are taking advantage of each other because I enjoy every minute of it. You are always considerate and not the least demanding. I'm fortunate to have this job."

He reached over to brush a lock of her hair away from her eyes. His nose began to run, and he momentarily turned away from her. She saw him wipe it with the back of his hand before he turned back. "Let's call it mutual admiration."

****

Mr. Stafford returned to work while Nora was still in the hospital. Each morning he stopped on his way to the office, again at lunchtime, then stayed to eat dinner with her before going home. As kind and solicitous as he was being, it made her uncomfortable. She thought

191

he was spending too much of his time with her, and she worried his life was disrupted and she knew how important routine was to him. Everything in his household was carefully planned and executed. Her accident veered from the plan, and that bothered her as much as her pain.

When she was ready to be discharged, the hospital's outpatient coordinator came to her room to discuss plans. "Is there a rehabilitation home I can go to until I can take care of myself?" Nora asked. "I'm a fast healer and I will push myself as hard as I dare."

Laughing long and loud the woman took a seat. "Are you serious?"

Nora certainly did not find it funny. Her expression must have made it obvious. "Miss Manning, Mr. Stafford and McNair have everything ready for you. A hospital bed was delivered to your home just this morning. A nurse will come in every day to check on your progress."

"But I don't have a home."

"Yes, you do, for as long as you want one," Ben said from the doorway.

She turned, half in shock but mostly surprised. "You can't keep me on while I'm still like this. I'm of no earthly use to you, and I don't know when I will be."

He rushed to her bedside. "I took it for granted you understood you are family."

She had an inordinate amount of pride and did not want charity. It made her uneasy. "I think it is best I recover in a rehabilitation center. I will only be a burden at your house."

His tone turned indignant. "I am not going to let you be just another patient in an impersonal rehabilitation center. I want you where you'll receive proper care and be comfortable. If you don't want to do it for yourself, do it for me. The house feels like a tomb since you have been gone."

They may not have verbally communicated much to each other in the past, but more was said in their silence than in words. They identified with each other on a level no one else understood. "But I don't know when I'll be one hundred percent."

"Nora, you were working for me when the accident happened. Consider this workman's compensation; in fact, it is. Discuss it with your attorney, he will confirm it," he said keeping his tone light.

"I don't have one of those either."

Ben pulled a chair up next to her bed and sat. "I guess we have been so worried about your recovery, we sadly neglected keeping you informed. In our defense, you were in no position to speak for yourself."

"I still don't know what you're talking about. Who are we?"

"Brian. Who else would be your attorney? He had a judge sign an order allowing him to act on your behalf while you were incapacitated."

She did not know quite how to react to the information. What did they find out about her while she was unconscious? How did they know to send her to the Veteran's Hospital? She was still in too much pain to think about it in detail.

The next time Brian stopped, she tried to feel him out about how much he knew. "Going home tomorrow, I hear," he said as he gave her a light kiss on the cheek.

"Mr. Stafford told me what you did for me. Thank you. I don't want to be any further bother or a burden to anyone. How will I be able to repay you?"

"Friends don't expect or want repayment, and I consider you a very good friend. There will be plenty of time for us to discuss anything you may want to tell me. Both as a friend and your lawyer, everything you say will remain confidential."

He knew about her; she was certain. She was equally certain Ben did not.

****

The following morning Molly appeared in her room. "Hi, I'll be your chauffeur today."

Nora smiled because Molly became a loyal friend. "How did you get stuck with the job?"

"It wasn't easy; the boys wanted to bring you home, but I told them sometimes you just need a woman's touch."

Nora sighed. "Thank you. They both are wonderful, but I am more comfortable with your help."

"I know. You're a very modest person and I appreciate that. We will get you home and tucked in. Then, you will do nothing but heal."

"From your lips to God's ear," Nora replied.

The nurses helped her into a wheelchair and escorted her to Molly's waiting car. She barely got to her feet with the aid of the nurse and Molly. She clung to the car door and allowed them to carefully position her in the front seat. She remembered the day she brought Ben home from the hospital after his appendectomy and how he did the same thing. If he was in a fraction of the pain she felt now, she did not know how he made it.

Molly helped Nora through the kitchen door when they were hit with confetti, a banner welcoming her home, and the honking of party favor horns. It was the stress reliever she needed. She expected something like that from Brian, but Ben was always so proper. It was a side of him unfamiliar to her.

"Okay, boys," Molly said. "Party's over; I'm getting her into bed."

Gingerly supported by Molly, Nora went to her room. She thought a hospital bed was unnecessary, but she quickly realized she needed the adjustments a normal bed did not offer. Just the short drive and walk into the house wore her out.

After Molly settled her in, Ben and Brian came in to see her. She was only awake for a few minutes. A nurse's aide arrived an hour later with little to do except assist Nora to the bathroom and adjust her pillows. Ben warned her not to run the risk of falling and reinjuring her ribs. She was still weak.

A woman hired from the employment agency came in everyday for two hours just to tidy up and prepare light meals. There was still a freezer filled with food which Nora had prepared and required little to defrost and reheat.

****

It was less than two weeks before Nora was going stir crazy; she believed the house and Ben were going to ruin without her personal supervision. The daily nurse was no longer necessary; she became mobile although far from able to do more than minor lifting. When the insurance check arrived for the replacement of her car, she felt able to go out to buy a new one. Molly drove her, but Ben insisted she buy a more substantial car. He was convinced her injuries were avoidable if she was driving a larger car or SUV. She found something she liked, but she was not cleared to drive yet; the dealer delivered it to the house. There was something about not having her own transportation, even if she was not supposed to drive, which unnerved her. It gave her a sense of being trapped. She was also uncomfortable watching someone else clean the house and her room. She sat in the garden whenever someone was cleaning so she did not have to watch.

****

Once Nora was safely home, Ben relaxed. He was accustomed to arriving home to a drink and hors d'oeuvres waiting for him, so he continued the practice. The only difference, he was making both and bringing them to her. His attempts were sorely inadequate by the standards Nora had set. He made a plate of cheese and crackers, a bourbon for him, and a glass of red wine for her. "It's your turn to be served," he said as he handed her the glass of wine.

"You don't have to do this. I know how busy you are." She smiled as she reached for the glass. "But I do need this wine."

He pulled a lawn chair up next to her for him to sit. "It's just good to have you home."

"It's good to be home, sir."

He was disappointed that the recent events did little to soften her formality. The more she recovered the more her reserve returned.

****

It was a warm sunny afternoon which found Nora relaxing in the yard when Brian came through the garden gate. She was surprised to see him in the middle of the day when he knew Ben was at the office. "You're looking really well," he said with a smile.

"I'm getting stronger every day and eager to get rid of the extra help. I feel guilty Mr. Stafford is spending unnecessary money because of me."

He gestured with a sweep of his hand. "He can afford it." Then hesitating, he added, "We really need to talk."

Her stomach flipped when he said the ominous word talk. "About what?" But she knew.

"The judge wouldn't just hand over a power of attorney to me unless he had substantial background information on you. It didn't take much more than a couple phone calls to get it. You need to tell Ben."

Nora felt flushed with panic. "You were acting as my lawyer, isn't everything confidential?"

He answered in a calm and reassuring voice. "Of course, it is. I've said nothing to no one, including my wife."

Her voice quivered and her hands began to shake. "Then what's the problem with letting sleeping dogs lie?"

"Because he is in love with you, and unless I'm greatly mistaken, you feel the same way. It's not that you're being dishonest with him; you're being dishonest with yourself."

"Can you blame me?" she asked barely squeaking out the words.

He took a deep breath and shook his head. "Blame is just about the last thing you need to do. I cannot tell you how badly I feel for you and everything you've been through, but it's in the past now."

"You can't possibly understand. It will never be in the past. Can I take time to think this over?"

"Nora, I will never say a word no matter what you

decide. I just hope you will decide on the truth. I fervently believe it is the only thing that will free you." He stood, leaned over, and kissed her on the forehead before leaving her to her thoughts.

She did think about it for the rest of the day and decided she needed to get away. She wanted to be alone to think without anyone's influence. Ben, Brian, and even Molly were completely devoted to her, but it was as crippling as her accident. When Ben came home, he did that which now became his routine and promptly went to check on her. "How are you doing?"

"The nurses' aide is going to take me to the doctor tomorrow. I expect he will clear me to drive again."

His brows furrowed and his voice became stern. "Don't be in a hurry."

She knew he was concerned for her welfare, but she thought he needed a break from her as much as she needed it for herself. "When we were at the cabin you said I was welcome to use it. Is the offer still open?"

"Of course, when did you want to go?"

"This weekend if I can drive."

"This weekend? Are you sure it's a good idea? If you insist, I will take you," he offered.

She shook her head. "Thank you, but no. I need a little time alone to regroup. You understand."

"I'm not sure I do. Here, you have people around to help you. I think it is ill advised, but you know what you need better than I."

When the weekend rolled around, she packed a small overnight bag and drove off in her new car. It was a far more pleasant trip in the early summer than it was in the winter. The trees were full, and the wildflowers were in bloom. She pulled up in front of the cabin and she viewed the lake and dock down the embankment. It instantly put her at ease. The quiet and fresh air were exactly what she needed. She gathered up the things she brought with her and headed inside; she was in for a surprise when she opened the door. The entire place was completely redecorated with new furniture, area rugs, and wall hangings. Everything was so perfect she was certain an interior decorator did it. She did not know if it was a decorating term, but she thought of it as *rustic cozy*. The cabin had a lighter look and feel. The heavily varnished log walls were lightly whitewashed, the furniture had overstuffed cushions, and all the appliances and dishes were replaced. It traded its mancave vibe for a softer presence. She opted to sleep on the new sofa bed rather than climb the loft stairs. She was physically strong enough, however prudent thinking prevailed. There was no point risking injury.

On her way up to the cabin, she had stopped at a small market in town and picked up a few groceries. As she put them in the refrigerator, she spotted the liquor cabinet. She laughed aloud knowing it was courtesy of Brian. There was every imaginable—high-end whiskey and thoughtfully selected expensive wines.

She went out the back door and headed for the dock. The weather was warm but not particularly hot. She meandered down the path to the dock. She gingerly lowered herself to its edge and took off her shoes to dip her feet in the cold lake. She took a deep breath of the fresh mountain air. It was something she took for granted until she broke her ribs; deep breaths were still painful. She sat there for an hour listening to the birds sing and watching fish jump out of the water. She cautiously pulled herself up and trekked back to the cabin. She stopped a couple of times because she was experiencing pain and shortness of breath. When she went inside, she found Ben sitting in an armchair. She stared at him in stunned silence. She certainly was not expecting to see him. She was frightened by him but not because she feared him. She was frightened by her feelings for him. It was those feelings which brought her to the secluded cabin.

"I never thought you'd drive up here."

He stood up, walked across the room to Brian's coveted liquor cabinet and poured himself a drink. He looked at her to see if she wanted one, but she nodded in the negative. "I hadn't intended on it. You barely left the house when I realized I needed to follow you."

"I promise I won't take the silver," she said with uncharacteristic sarcasm.

He sneered. "If you want it, you're welcome to take it."

"I miss the paper plates and broken glass on the floor," she said to avoid dealing with why he was there in the first place.

He strolled across the floor with his drink in hand. "Looks a little different, doesn't it?"

"It's beautiful."

"I did it because of you."

Chapter Nineteen

Nora remained silent while Ben explained himself. "When we were here during the winter, I realized how important this place really is to me. It had a long history in my heart, but I stayed away because of the more recent one."

"I don't think I understand," she said clutching the arm of the sofa to lower herself down.

"My ex-wife and I used to bring Elizabeth up here nearly every weekend. She loved it. When she died, I stopped loving everything which made her happy because she'd never experience it again. Then when I was telling you about my father, who also loved this place, it was my fondest memory we had his last days here. I didn't know how I could have a similar experience with both, with two divergent emotions. I guess it was because my father, although not old, still had a lifetime behind him, while Lizzie did not."

"She had a lifetime; it just wasn't the length you planned."

"I know that now, but I didn't then. There are so many things I have learned about myself recently."

He walked over to Nora and knelt before her. "I don't know when this happened, but I now realize how important you are to me. You made me face reality. I was angry, hurt, closed off from anything and anyone who wanted to pull me from my grief. I let it become the thing which defined me; then you came into my life. Call it luck; call it providence, but you were there. I was half out of my mind when I thought you would die from the accident. You have shown me a way to let go of my grief. There were so many amazing things about Lizzie's life and the only thing I concentrated on was her death. I did her a great injustice and you helped me see that."

She placed her hand on his cheek and spoke in a tender voice. "You give me too much credit, you were ready."

He stood and looked down at her imploring, "Let me do as much for you. What are you running from?"

She turned her eyes away and stared at the floor. "I'm not worth your effort to find out."

"I don't believe that. I wouldn't feel this way if it were true." His voice was filled with anger, not at her but the notion she was unworthy.

She motioned for him to sit beside her and the expression on her face was so grief stricken he only wanted to comfort her. He gently kissed her lips and when she did not pull away, he pulled her close to his chest. It was something he wanted to do many times but never dared. She seemed so emotionally fragile he was afraid to even try.

His kiss changed them forever. She closed her eyes and rested in his arms. He wanted the moment to last forever. It felt right, but he also felt her tense up and pull back to look him in the face. "You wanted to know what I am running from—myself. Unfortunately, everywhere I go, my past goes with me."

His tone was dismissive. "Nora, we all have a past. I know enough about your character to know what a truly remarkable person you are. I want a chance to prove it to you. I want a life with you. Nothing can be so horrendous we can't work through it together."

She got to her feet and walked to the other side of the room, turned, and faced him. "I can't be with you, not the way you want."

Ben went to her. He wanted to embrace her again, but she stepped back. Then an upsetting thought came to him. "Oh, no! You're still married, aren't you?"

"No, Philip is dead." Her voice trailed off.

He was devastated for her. "I'm so sorry, but I'm not surprised. Your mother-in-law seemed to have genuine affection for you. If there had been a messy divorce, she was not likely to have come looking for you."

It was the first time Nora smiled. "She's been like a mother to me. I have known her most of my life, and my father-in-law has been wonderful too. I thank God every day for them."

"You're probably their connection to their son. I can understand why they don't want to lose that."

She turned her back to him and bowed her head. "They don't need that kind of connection; trust me."

"Please start at the beginning so I can understand?" He took her arm and led her back to the sofa and Nora asked him for a drink. He brought out a bottle of wine, but she shook her head, he pointed at the whiskey, she nodded. He thought it must be something horrendous because he never saw her drink whiskey. He needed one too and poured himself another.

As she took a sip, she seemed detached as she spoke, like she was reading from a script. "Philip was my high school boyfriend. He was everything I was not, funny, handsome, popular, and the high school football star. The only thing I *was* that he was not, was a good student. The coach asked if I would tutor him to make him eligible to play in the state championship. For whatever reason he really liked me. I was shy and awkward, and I couldn't believe he wanted to be with me when nearly every girl in our class drooled over him." She began to smile, obviously, thinking about him back in high school. Ben did not interrupt, he just waited for her to continue in her own time, in her own manner.

"After high school I attended the Boston Conservatory of Music, and because he was not academically inclined, he decided to join the army. We got together when he was on leave and I was home from school, but it was never anything serious. When I graduated and returned home there were not a lot of jobs for music majors. My mother worked at the same high school I graduated from and helped me get a part time teaching position. I supplemented my income by working at a local restaurant. That's where I realized how much I enjoyed cooking."

"Philip was deployed to the Middle East and when he returned, he wanted to get married. It was about the same time my dad started having health issues, possibly from exposure to Agent Orange during the Vietnam War. My parents moved to a drier climate, and after Philip and I married, they turned the house over to us. It was an enormous old brick Victorian house at the edge of town. It was always too big for the two of us. We only lived in part of it, but it had been in my family for generations. It was my father who suggested I turn it into an inn."

Ben interrupted her, asking with astonishment, "The inn you worked at belonged to you?"

"Yes," she answered in a monotone then droned on. "It was one of the last things my father did before he died; helping me renovate it. We turned the top floor into living quarters for Philip and me. He was deployed again. The inn was a rewarding distraction, especially after my father died, and shortly thereafter, my mother. Fortunately, my in-laws were there for me, and I could not have asked for any better people to be a part of my family."

Suddenly the missing pieces of the puzzle who Nora was came together for Ben. Her husband's military service was why she volunteered at the hospital. It was the reason she had veteran's insurance and why the general at the old man's funeral knew her. Ben gasped predicting the reason for her pain. "Oh, Nora, I'm so sorry; he was killed in action."

She stared at him, tears in her eyes but her voice clear. "No, he was killed by me."

Ben felt every ounce of breath rush from his lungs. He was dizzy from shock. He paused while he composed himself. He didn't know what to say to her. What can he say when the person he has grown to love says she killed her husband? However, this kind gentle woman sitting before him, a woman he had in his home for the past year, a woman who had cared for him when he needed her and volunteered at the hospital, certainly was not responsible for someone's death. There must be an explanation, and he patiently waited for it.

Nora's eyes were trained on him. Ben sensed she was gauging his reaction on whether to continue. He needed the truth and remained deadpan. He did not want her to have any reason not to trust him. "I doubt you woke up one day and said to yourself, 'I think I'll kill my husband today.' I know you too well to believe there was anything malicious in your heart."

"How can you be so confident. I was a stranger who showed up at your door. What do you really know about me? Malicious or not, does it matter? He died at my hands."

His voice rose to a higher octave. "Of course, it matters. There is an enormous difference between being the instrument of someone's death and culpability for it. I don't suppose for one instance you believe I think you intentionally killed him."

"I lied to you."

Ben slid to his knees in front of her as she sat on the sofa. He took both her hands in his. "You never lied to me."

"I was in your house under false pretense. I knew no one would ever hire me if they knew what I did."

He squeezed her hands so hard she pulled them free. "I don't think what you did is even a lie by omission. If it were true, I am equally as guilty by not speaking of Lizzy."

She sniffed as her nose ran. "It's not even remotely the same thing."

"It is exactly the same thing. Each of us was in pain and did not want to discuss it. It was eating me alive, and I wasn't even aware of it until you came into my life. I'm not a fool, Nora, I knew you were hiding something."

"Yet you never asked? Were you afraid to know?"

Her question struck a nerve in him, and he cringed. Brian said the same thing to him when Nora first arrived. He admitted to himself he did not want anything to disrupt their lives. He was equally confident in her character, whatever it was didn't matter. "Not afraid to know, just afraid you might leave if I delved into it."

She seemed to understand his concern and continued to tell him about her husband. "Philip had already completed two tours in the Middle East with no major incidents. Don't get me wrong, he saw plenty of death and destruction, but he remained physically unharmed. It was his third tour which changed all our lives forever."

She looked so distraught, he asked, "Do you need a break? You don't have to finish right now if this is too difficult for you."

She shook her head. "No, I have started, I have to finish. Philip was on patrol when a suicide bomber came at him and his men. He threw himself in the bomber's path and when the bomb exploded, he was seriously injured, but he saved all his men."

Ben bowed his head and exclaimed, "Good Lord!"

"We honestly did not think he'd live. His injuries were so catastrophic. He very nearly lost his legs, but they were able to save them."

"Was he able to walk again?"

"Yes, but he was in the hospital for the better part of a year between his legs and internal injuries. Marjorie, the woman I eventually sold my inn to, assumed management of it while I went to stay near the Veteran's Hospital. His parents were regular visitors. I can't tell you how hard it was on them watching him struggle every day."

"That's why you knew so much about changing

bandages and drain tubes," Ben stated rather than asked.

"He wanted to come home so badly, I learned as much as I could to take care of him. It was mentally important for all of us to try to establish a normal life. At first when we brought him home, the relief he felt was almost euphoric. He hadn't been home for long periods of time before, so now he had the opportunity to help me with the inn. He never talked about his war experience. He was starting to regain a little of the vivaciousness I remember from our old high school days. He talked with guests, drank coffee with the locals, and even volunteered coaching a little league team."

There was trepidation in Ben's voice. "But?"

"It was all an act," she said sadly. "He was far from all right. He felt he owed it to me and his parents to let us think he was the person we needed him to be. He started having nightmares. He claimed he didn't remember them, but the things he shouted were always about being shot at, or explosions."

"He was suffering from Post Traumatic Stress Disorder?"

"Big time," she said. "Then one day he was contacted by the army and told he was being awarded the Congressional Medal of Honor for his actions which led to his injuries. We thought receiving the highest honor a soldier can receive might help to validate his feelings and find some peace of mind."

Nora got up and walked to the liquor cabinet, poured another drink, and stared out the window. Ben said nothing. She was obviously trying to put her thoughts together. She returned to her seat beside him.

"Philip, his parents, and I all went to the White House. We met the president; he received his medal with the other members of his unit there to cheer him on. We returned to our quiet, uneventful lives."

"Is that why the general at Mr. Pirelli's funeral knew you?" Ben asked.

She nodded. "He was in command at the time and aware of what happened. I never knew much about him. When he returned to the States, he came to visit Philip once."

"I assume the medal didn't help."

"No, in fact it made it worse. He felt unworthy and became more depressed and filled with anger. At first it was directed at silly, inane things like the lawnmower not starting or a flat tire. His reactions were overblown for the circumstance, but I ignored them. Then it escalated into the public. If someone walked across the street when he was driving down the road, he would roll down his window and scream obscenities at them. He'd pound on the hood of their car if they beat him to a parking space. Naturally, having been awarded the Medal of Honor he was a hometown hero and granted a lot of leeway. He wasn't like that all the time. When he was having better days where he was able to understand his behavior, he would go to the VA hospital for a few days. They would try different medications and therapy."

Ben did not know what to say nor do, he just let her talk. He hoped unburdening herself was therapeutic.

"He started to have bouts of paranoia and believed everything was a conspiracy. His parents had the most influence over him, but they even lost what little ability they had to reason with him. It was when he started to hallucinate, the real problems began. On two occasions he attacked me while we were sleeping believing I was an enemy combatant trying to kill him."

Ben was horrified. "What did he do to you?"

She swallowed hard, took deep steady breaths, and said, "He beat me to the point I had to be hospitalized."

In a shrill voice Ben asked, "Why didn't you leave him?"

She sounded resigned to his treatment. "I couldn't. He wasn't intentionally being abusive; he didn't know who I was. When he snapped back to reality, he was hysterical by what he had done. The police were regulars at the inn, and it did little to enhance my business. He was my husband and sacrificed so much for his country I couldn't or wouldn't give up on him."

"It wasn't as if it were abandonment," Ben reasoned.

"Would you have left?"

He was silent for a moment. "Probably not. I'd think things might get better."

"That's exactly what I thought, but ironically the people who didn't think that were his parents. They wanted him to come and live with them to keep me safe. His father told me he was their responsibility. They brought him into the world, and they thought he was their obligation to care for. Philip refused to consider it, and I didn't feel right about it either. They were getting on in years and did not need the kind of volatility which came with caring for him."

"I don't understand why the VA didn't do more."

"It's a gray area. If he was arrested and processed through the courts, they had the authority to do something, but who wants to prosecute a Medal of

Honor recipient? The police didn't, and I certainly didn't. Eventually I was forced to close the inn. I couldn't very well run a public oriented business under the circumstances."

"That must have broken your heart. How did you survive? What did you live on?" Ben asked.

She waved her hand in a dismissive manner. "Money was the least of my problems. Don't forget my parents gave me the house. Even after all the remodeling we did in it was paid for and my parents left me a little money as well. Philip was also receiving full disability benefits; we were fine in financial regard. What bothered me the most was the solitude and disconnect from once having a successful business to a large vacant building. Meeting new people and expressing myself through cooking was my way of coping. When I closed it down, it was just Philip and me. It had to be that way for everyone's sake."

Ben was getting anxious, not for himself but for Nora. "How long did you live that way?"

"About six months. I came home one evening and found him sitting on the floor with a hunting knife in his hand. All his guns were confiscated for our safety, but anyone can get a knife." She closed her eyes and swallowed hard as she described the scene. "He was just rocking back and forth in a trance, sliding the blade side of the knife up and down his arm. Sometimes he even nicked himself and watched the blood trickle on the floor. He became aware of my presence and said, 'I should just plunge this damn thing into my chest and be done with it.' I tried talking to him in a soothing voice. I told him everything would be fine. We'd get help for him. You know all the things you say to calm someone down."

"Why didn't you call for help?"

He clearly has never been in her situation. "I didn't dare back away at that point. He might react to having his plan interrupted and do it anyway. I really thought my best course of action was to continue talking him down. I sat in front of him to make eye contact and I thought he was responding. As I reached out to carefully pull the knife from his hand, he snapped."

Ben was not sure he even wanted to hear the rest, but he knew he must. He was the one who forced this discussion. He squirmed uncomfortably on the sofa cushions.

"In his mind he was back in Afghanistan, and someone was trying to disarm him. He lunged at me with such savagery every bit of adrenalin I had reacted. We wrestled with the knife, but he was much stronger than I, and the next thing I knew I was bleeding."

Ben turned white and his voice shook. "That's why you have the scar down the length of your stomach."

"How did you know about that?"

"I saw it by accident when you were fixing the kitchen curtains. Your shirt rose when you had your hands above your head. I knew it didn't look like a surgical scar."

His observation did not deter her from continuing her story. "Somehow the knife slipped from his hand. The only thing working in my favor was his leg injuries. He was unable to get up as quickly as I, even with my injuries. I started to run when he grabbed my pant leg. I fell back down and found my hand near the knife; I grasped it and blindly plunged it into him. I wasn't aiming, just trying to get away, but the target the knife hit was his heart. He was dead instantly."

Nora was reciting the events in a robotic manner. She seemed detached from them, and Ben clearly understood why. It was like a horror movie, only she lived it.

"I was in the hospital for weeks. His parents made all the funeral arrangements. The army sent a representative and they conducted a full military funeral burying him in Arlington. Naturally, I was unable to get the closure I needed because I was still hospitalized."

"Certainly, you were never charged with anything."

Her eyes met his and he recognized the agony in them. "No, it was never even considered. His behavior and the earlier beatings I received were well documented. The district attorney convened a grand jury to hear the case, but it was for my protection as a matter of law."

Ben still needed clarification. "I understand the horrific nature of what you went through, but if no charges were ever filed, why did you run away and live in such secrecy? Your in-laws certainly never believed it was anything but self defense."

"You can't fully understand unless you have been brought up in a small town."

He nodded. "Oh, they never really believed you were innocent."

She looked shocked and exclaimed, "No! It was just the opposite. They were so kind and sympathetic they were drowning me in pity. I reopened the inn and business boomed, especially the restaurant. The townspeople wanted to show their support for me."

He looked at her with total confusion on his face.

"So, what was the problem? They cared about you. I think it's commendable they were so supportive."

She started nervously rubbing her hands together and her feet repeatedly tapped the floor. "It was awful. It may sound terrible to say, but it was. I was always 'poor Nora,' or worse yet I would see children point and say to their friends, 'that's the woman who killed her husband because he was crazy.' "

"I tried to conduct business as usual, but it was pointless. Everything was a reminder of Philip. One day, when I had enough, I asked Marjorie if she wanted to buy the inn. She said she would run it for as long as I liked but didn't want me to make so big of a decision, but I insisted. Once the papers were signed, I got in my car and just started driving until dark. That's how I ended up in Bartholomew. The rest you know."

"How long ago did he die?"

"It has been over two years. The longest two years of my life." She had a complete breakdown and started to cry unconsolably. Ben held her close, gently caressing her hair. He let her shed the tears she had bottled up inside for so long. His shirt was soaked by the time she fell asleep in his arms out of sheer emotional exhaustion. He was disgusted over all the years he squandered in useless self-pity after losing his daughter. It was a tragic loss which he knew he would carry with him for the rest of his life. His little girl left this world with the love and the security only parents can provide. What Nora endured and the courage with which she did it was something he was incapable of empathizing.

He carefully extricated himself from her and positioned her on the sofa with a comfortable pillow and covered her with a blanket. His heart was aching for her. He stood watch over her; when he was certain she would not wake until morning, he went to bed in the loft. Ben wanted to sleep too, but he was consumed with her pain and the desire to relieve her of it. He felt running away was not the right choice for her when there were so many people who cared about her. He did, however, completely understand why she fled. In a sense he did the same thing, only his was an emotional escape. Everything was out in the open now; he thought they could move forward. He eventually closed his eyes and fell fast asleep.

Chapter Twenty

The dawn was breaking when Ben awoke. He went downstairs to check on Nora, but she was not on the sofa. He thought she was in the bathroom, but the door was open. He began to panic when he saw her overnight bag was not on the floor. A brief glance out the window did not reveal her car in the driveway. He slammed his fist down on the countertop and shouted, "Damn it." He was furious with himself. She ran once before, why didn't it occur to him history was likely to repeat itself? He felt certain she returned to the house. She still had all her clothing and personal effects in her room.

Ben broke every speed limit posted between the cabin and his house. If luck were with him, he would catch her before she had a chance to leave. He wanted to stop her, reason with her. He was not lucky. The kitchen door was unlocked. He went straight for her room, but it was stripped of every personal item. He dropped heavily upon her bed trying to get inside her mind to figure out where she went. It worried him even Nora may not have that answer. She left her home before with no destination in mind.

It finally dawned on him Brian must have uncovered something about her, so he drove to his house. He repeatedly rang the bell and pounded on the door. From the front porch Ben could hear someone running down the stairs. When the door was flung open Brian was dressed only in his underwear. "Ben," he said with astonishment. "What are you doing here at this unholy hour?"

Ben pushed past him into the house as Brian slammed the door shut behind him. "You knew, didn't you?" he shouted, grabbing him by his t-shirt.

Brian grasped Ben's wrist and thrust him backward. "Come in and calm down."

Molly rushed down the stairs. "What's going on? Ben, why are you here?" Brian waved her off.

Brian evoked his best lawyerly demeanor. "What is it you think I know?"

Ben's nostrils flared. "About Nora, don't play games with me. She's gone and I need to find her."

"Calm down and tell me what happened."

Ben paced back and forth, running his hand through his unkempt hair. "She wanted to go to the cabin yesterday and I knew something was bothering her, so I followed her. She finally told me everything."

"Excuse me, I'm not trying to be coy, but just what is *everything*?" Brian asked.

"Everything: where she came from, who she is, how she killed her husband," he said with irritation and panic in his voice.

They heard Molly gasp. "Killed her husband?"

Brian turned to his wife. "I'll explain later."

"I couldn't tell you, Ben. I was bound by lawyer-client confidentiality. I did tell her she needed to be honest with you."

"Ohhh"— Ben exaggerated the word— "she told me all right. We have to find her. I don't think she's well enough to be on her own. I cannot even begin to know what her mental state is. Where would she go?"

Brian grabbed his laptop computer and accessed Nora's file. "I'd start with her hometown."

"She left there, why would she go back?" Ben asked.

"Maybe because she has friends there. Who does she trust?"

"Her in-laws. They were very close. I met her mother-in-law once."

Brian's head shot up. "You did? When was that?"

Waving him off he said, "Veteran's Day. It doesn't matter."

"You knew she had in-laws and never said anything to me?"

"Yes, and you didn't tell me about what happened to her."

"That's different." Brian was indignant. "So, you know about the Bauers."

"Not their names, just that she was married or still was for all I knew. We didn't talk about it back then."

Brian's research never went as far as Nora's in-laws, it was not necessary because they were not blood relatives. He did have the address of the inn and jotted it down for Ben.

"I'd try there first. Do you want me to go with you?"

Ben's pupils dilated making them black and menacing. "No, you've done quite enough."

He realized he had no reason to be angry with his friend, but he needed to take it out on someone. He dashed out of Brian's house gripping the slip of paper with the address. His car tires spun as he raced down the driveway to find Nora.

****

When the door closed behind Ben, Molly asked, "Do you have a story you want to tell me?"

There was no longer any reason for confidentiality, so Brian told his wife what he knew. Molly inhaled and put her hands to her face. "That poor woman. No wonder she was so reclusive. I'd do the same thing."

He looked at his wife with pure love in his eyes. "Maybe I didn't do the right thing in keeping her secret."

She embraced him. "I don't know what other choice you had. You were bound by confidentiality."

"If you can forgive me for saying nothing, I have to believe Ben can."

****

Nora only slept briefly in the cabin. When she heard Ben go to bed in the loft, she waited a while to ensure he was asleep, then slipped out. She had hours of advance time to get away. It was not a lack of trust in Ben's ability to understand and accept what had happened to her, it was her own inability to do the same. She did not want another individual to share her burden. She felt unworthy of his love, so she left. She had no plans just as she had none when she made her first retreat. The difference between then and now was her health. She knew starting over must be postponed until she healed. She needed a place where it was possible. She did not want to burden them, but her in-laws' home was the logical place to recover. She kept her promise and phoned them on a regular basis just to assure them she was fine. They did not, however, know about her accident. In their advanced years it was a burden she kept from them. They were not supportive of her leaving, but they always respected her right to do what she must to cope. She headed her car in their direction.

It was midafternoon when she arrived at the Bauers'. They lived in a small ranch house just outside the village limits of Darling less than five minutes from the inn. Nora rang the bell. Her mother-in-law answered and nearly fell over when she saw her. She moved toward Nora to embrace her, but Nora put her hands up to stop her. Her mother-in-law halted as she stared at Nora and her hands went to her lips. She saw the healing scars and missing hair. She cried, "What happened to you?"

"I was in a serious car accident. I hate to burden you, but can I stay here until I'm better?" Nora asked in a pleading tone.

Her father-in-law hobbled in leaning heavily on his cane. "Pat, for goodness sake help the child to a chair."

Nora was grateful to be sitting with her feet up and not driving endlessly in a car. She looked around the homey and comfortable house where she spent countless happy days. Above the fireplace hung a framed photograph of Philip, Nora, his parents, and the President of the United States after receiving his Medal of Honor. Beneath the photo on the mantel was the flag which draped his coffin when he was buried in Arlington. Traditionally it was presented to the widow, but when Nora was not well enough to attend, it was given to his parents. They needed to honor him despite what happened. Nora was fine with it. She was too haunted by the past to do the same thing. She wanted her in-laws to do whatever brought them peace of mind.

Her father-in-law used his cane to help lower

himself into a chair opposite her. "You're a daughter to us, you know that. You have a home with us for as long as you like."

Pat started fussing over her. She put a pillow behind her back, brought her a cup of herbal tea, and examined every scar on her body. It was then Nora realized how truly selfish it was to run away. She still believed it was the right thing for her, but she was not the only person devastated by Philip's death. In many ways it was worse for them. Nora's scars were more visible than the Bauers'.

She did not know if they were happy to see her or if they needed the distraction of taking care of her. Either way she needed them, and they needed her, but there was still a dark cloud hanging overhead.

"Wouldn't that man you worked for help you?" Pat asked as she arranged a light throw across Nora's legs.

There was a pain in her heart even though her words did not reveal it. "Mr. Stafford was wonderful about the whole thing. He arranged for nursing care and paid any bills which were not covered by the insurance. He felt obligated because I was running an errand for him at the time."

"Then what's the problem?" her father-in-law asked.

"Don," his wife admonished him. "It's none of our business."

Despite herself, Nora smiled. She missed the old days when they were constantly bickering in a good-natured way. "I didn't feel right about staying. I can't do much for a while and he doesn't need the burden of me in his house when he can hire someone else."

No further questions were asked by the Bauers. If

there was more to the story, they never asked. "You just relax and let us take care of you," Pat said as she fussed over her.

Nora was worried about her sudden reappearance. "Can we keep my visit quiet? I don't want it known around town I'm back. I just do not need that kind of attention right now."

Pat replied, "Of course, dear. The only thing we ask of you is not to disappear again without telling us. It was so difficult not knowing where you were for so long."

Nora bowed her head in shame, when Don added, "You had to do what you had to do. Often, grief and logic are mortal enemies. Philip couldn't help what he became, and we've finally made peace with it, we only wish the same for you."

Nora gazed into the old man's eyes. "I have made peace with it too. He sacrificed everything, and I don't even try to rationalize why it isn't fair. I don't know how I killed someone I loved so much."

Pat went to her, putting her arms around her without hurting her battered body. "You didn't kill the man you loved any more than he attacked his wife. They were two different people. I know you have a tough time making sense of it, but it's the sad truth. Why don't you get some rest, and we can talk later. There is nothing further to discuss today."

She escorted Nora to Philip's old bedroom. She hesitated before entering. She was not sure she wanted to go inside. She need not have worried. Where there was a shrine to Philip's service for his country in the living room, the Bauers completely redecorated his bedroom. Gone were the high school banners, model cars, and music posters. It was an ordinary guest room. Pat pointed to an old steamer trunk in the corner. "I put everything in there. Those are memories I want to revisit when I need them, they don't need to be on display."

Nora now understood Ben did the same thing with his daughter. She never saw a single article belonging to her displayed around the house. It was his attic which held the memories he revisited.

She was more fatigued than she realized and quickly fell asleep. She had no idea where she was going or what she might do with the rest of her life. She was most comfortable with the idea of being alone despite her earlier attempt ending in disaster.

She hoped for Ben's sake, that he realized she was too emotionally damaged to have a relationship with anyone. It was not fair, despite the truth she loved him. If she were in his life, it certainly meant heartache.

****

It was dark by the time Ben found the inn. He drove around the parking lot to the back and did not see Nora's car. He had prayed she was there, but he was not going to give up easily. The new owner might be able to help him. He was now on Nora's turf and her friends may be protective of her. He needed to spend the night somewhere, thinking it might as well be at the inn. It was quaint with its wide porches, gazebos, and the intricate millwork. He imagined a spectacular interior. He was not disappointed; the charm extended inside. He thought to himself it must have been a wonderful place for her to grow up. The front section of the house contained the public rooms with books, games, and a huge fireplace. The walls were adorned with framed photos of the town and surrounding areas during the period the house was built. He took the time to look at them. Off to one side was the dining room. It was not large, but it accommodated fifteen tables of various sizes. He was unable to see the kitchen he knew was important to Nora. Beside the grand staircase leading to the guest rooms was a small office nook where a young girl sat playing video games on the computer. Ben approached her. "Do you have any rooms? I don't have a reservation."

She clicked off the game and gave him her full attention. He imagined she was bored sitting there, but maybe she had other duties as well. "Yes, we do. The busy season doesn't start until the end of the month. We have four available. Anything in particular?"

"Something simple; I'll only be here for the night."

She handed him a key. "Second floor, first door to the left."

He climbed the stairs and found his room. He asked for something simple and he got it. Although clean, it was sparse. It consisted of a double bed, upholstered chair, and a dresser. They did have the amenities of Wi-Fi and cable television, but the inn catered to people trying to get away. It struck Ben as ironic that Nora was the one who had to get away. Strategically a sink, toilet, and shower were crammed into what once was a large closet. Certainly, having a private bathroom was more important than a closet. Nevertheless, it was pleasant.

He picked up the brochures which highlighted area points of interest and flipped through them. His blood ran cold when he found mention of the town being home of Congressional Medal of Honor recipient Philip

Bauer. There was no mention beyond the stated fact of it being his hometown.

He took a shower and climbed into bed going over in his mind what to say to her if he found her. She could not hide forever. If necessary, he would do exactly what her in-laws did and hire a private investigator. His main concern was her mental and physical health.

The next morning, he ventured down to the dining room and sat at a small table near the porch. Only one other table was occupied but it was still early. He wanted to see if it was possible to glean any kind of information about Nora. He was not hungry, but the coffee and homemade sweet rolls were enticing. An elderly woman came to the table and poured him a cup of coffee. "Did you have a restful night?"

Taking a sip of his coffee he replied, "Yes, it's a lovely inn. A friend of mine stayed here a few years ago and told me if I was ever up this way to make sure I ate dinner here. He said it was the best meal he ever ate." He hoped his subterfuge was subtle enough to gain information about Nora.

The woman had no reason to think he was lying. "That is nice praise. We strive to do our best."

Coy in his question, Ben asked, "Are you the owner?"

"Yes, I am." She extended her hand. "I'm Marjorie."

Ben tried his best to feign confusion. "I don't think that was the name my friend gave me who did the cooking."

"It was probably Nora," she answered.

"That sounds more familiar," he said in normal conversational tone. He was trying not to sound like he was interrogating her. "I will have to make sure I stick around for dinner. I don't want to miss one of her meals."

She topped off his coffee mug. "Nora has moved on, but she left us all her best recipes. You won't be disappointed."

"I'm sure I won't. She is probably a chef at some fancy restaurant," Ben said in a matter-of-fact tone.

"Wouldn't surprise me," was the only answer he received. She certainly was no gossip and the reason Nora trusted her.

His only other choice was to find her in-laws. It was not something he wanted to do, but he knew no other clues to her whereabouts. If he started asking questions around town, he may cause unnecessary talk and speculation. The easiest thing to do was check for a listing in the phone directory. Fortunately, it yielded the Bauers' address and phone number. It was still early, so he did a drive-by of their house. To his enormous relief he spotted Nora's car in the driveway. Now the only thing he must figure out is the best way to approach her while being sensitive to her in-laws.

Chapter Twenty-One

Nora's painful body stirred her awake the following morning. It took her several minutes to acclimate. At first, she was confused by her surroundings. It was not unusual; she had the same experience when in the hospital. Her life had dramatically changed in the last month. She would give anything to return to the orderly and impersonal life she lived over the past year. She heard a gentle rap on her door. It slowly opened to reveal her mother-in-law. "How are you feeling, dear?"

Nora grimaced as she propped herself up on a pillow. She hated how stiff and sore she was, and the long drive only aggravated her condition. "I'm getting better every day," she reassured her.

Pat smiled and nodded. "It will take time. Let Don and I pamper you a little."

Nora gave her a weak smile. "I don't have much choice."

"You have nothing but choices. You're a young woman with a lot of life ahead of you. Your body is not the only thing that needs to heal; so, does your spirit."

Nora hung her head in despair. "Do you suppose it's possible to send my mind away for a while, at least until my body can heal? I can't handle much more."

"You tried that once. I'm afraid for good or bad they're a package deal. You are a lot stronger than you think." The kindness in her voice made Nora want to cry. A tear trickled down her cheek.

"I am a coward. I wasn't able to even face the people who care about me."

"You needed to sort things out. I didn't understand at first. Don and I felt like we let you down."

Nearly gasping for breath, she replied, "How can you even say that? You were the best parents to both Philip and me."

"We didn't protect you. In our hearts we honestly believed Philip was incapable of harming any of us. He put you in the hospital twice and nearly killed you. Don and I live with it every day."

"You can't blame yourselves. We only related to Philip as the person we knew prior to his injuries. Even with everything I went through with him, I never thought it might lead to his death."

"I'm not concerned with any of it right now. We have tortured ourselves for two years and it must stop; today is as good a day as any."

Nora wanted to bury her head in her pillow and forget the past two years. "I don't know how."

"You'll learn; we'll learn together. The first step is getting healthy again. We can put the other pieces together later."

Nora nodded, still too emotionally tired and physically incapacitated to do anything else. Pat left her alone while she dressed and then she joined her in-laws in the kitchen. She gingerly pulled out a chair and lowered herself down. She looked over at her father-in-law and it broke her heart to see how badly his health had deteriorated in the past year. It redoubled her assertion she had been selfish. When they needed her most, she ran away to avoid facing her ghosts.

"Eat something, you're beginning to look like a skeleton," Don said.

She smiled at his concern. "I'm really not very hungry."

Pat placed a bowl of freshly prepared berries before her. "At least have a few of these."

Nora picked at the fruit but was barely able to swallow them. It was ridiculous, but she felt she was too fatigued to chew. "Would you mind if I took my cup of tea and sit in the yard for a while?"

Don tapped her gently with his cane and said, "The sun will do you better than sitting around here with a couple of old codgers."

****

Ben waited no longer; at eleven o'clock he rang the Bauers' doorbell and paused frozen with increasing anxiety. Mrs. Bauer answered and stood staring at his familiar face. "Mr. Stafford," she said pulling the door open wider.

"I apologize for just showing up at your door, but I need to see Nora. It's urgent."

She motioned for him to come in. "I did the same thing to you for the same reason. Please, come in." She pointed at her husband. "This is my husband, Don."

Don tried to get to his feet with the help of his cane, but Ben quickly stopped him. "Please don't get up on my account." He went over to shake his hand.

"It's very nice to meet you; have a seat, Mr. Stafford," he said.

"Thank you," Ben replied as he pulled out a chair. He was impatient to see Nora, but he had just imposed himself on them. They had the right to speak with him to inquire about his presence in their home.

"Nora is resting in the backyard. I will get her for you," Pat said as she headed for the back door.

Her husband called out, "Just a minute, Pat, I'd like to have a few words with Mr. Stafford first."

Ben did not know what to expect. Nora told him how kind they were so he assumed they would be reasonable people. Don continued, "Why are you here? I cannot believe you'd drive all this way unannounced to inquire of her health."

"Actually, I did, but I also want her to come back with me."

Don was abrupt in his tone. "She's in no condition to go back to work."

Ben sighed. "There has been too much secrecy for too long on both our parts. We have finally broken the silence, which was keeping us from living our lives, or at least I have. I want that for Nora too. I've come to know and respect her. We each, in a sense, were living in our own prisons. It's time to be paroled."

"You're in love with her," Pat said.

Ben looked at her with pleading eyes to understand. "I want you to know there has never, ever been even the most minuscule impropriety by either of us. She has never even called me by my first name. The formality which exists between us is what led to a friendship and deeper compassion for the other. To answer your question, yes, I am in love with her. I cannot imagine my life without her. I didn't expect it to happen, I wasn't looking for it, but it happened."

Ben feared Mr. Bauer did not believe him. "Ben, I will call you that even if Nora has not. I know more about you than you do yourself. Do you think for one minute we would go to the extent of hiring a private investigator to find Nora and not also investigate the man whose house she was living in? We know your reputation and character. If we thought it was necessary, we would have dragged her out your door kicking and screaming."

Ben was stunned; he did not have the slightest inkling they went to such an extent to investigate him. It was almost unnerving. At the same time, he did not blame them. Nora was all they had, and her safety was paramount. He felt the same sense of responsibility.

"I never knew I was being investigated."

Mr. Bauer smiled. "That was the point. I was less concerned it might offend you if you found out than I was you'd learn Nora's secret. She was at least in a safe environment, even if it was not with us."

"It must have taken a lot of self control not to approach her."

"We didn't dare. This may sound like an odd contradiction, but Nora is a fragile rock. She will do what needs to be done with no trepidation. Her heart is so big she feels every emotion tenfold of the average person. We knew she was safe with you and gave her the space and time to reflect on her life. You are right; it took every ounce of reserve to not contact her. If it had not been for another episode with my heart, Pat would not have come to your home. We didn't want her to run again."

Ben pointed out the obvious. "But she did."

"There were millions of places she may have gone. She had enough money to convalesce anywhere. She chose to come home; the first place you'd look for her. Am I right?" Don asked.

Ben shook his head. "It was the only place I knew to start. Do you suppose she wanted me to find her?"

"Maybe not consciously, but yes. If you are in love with her, tell her and take her away from here. There is nothing left for her in this town except painful memories."

"You approve? I know that's of supreme importance to her. These are extraordinary circumstances," Ben said. He was not ignorant of the fact they were making an enormous personal sacrifice by freeing her from any obligation to them.

"We approve of anything or anyone who can give that precious child the peace of mind and happiness she deserves."

There were tears in both Pat and Don's eyes and Ben never had more respect for anyone than he did the Bauers. It took exceptional people to rise above the tragedies they suffered.

"Go talk to her. Make her understand what's in your heart. If she can stop blaming herself long enough, she will realize what's best for her," Don said motioning toward the patio door.

Ben hesitated as he exited the house. Nora's back was to him as she was sitting in a lounge chair. He approached her like he might a wounded pet, carefully and speaking in a soft voice. "Nora," he said.

She turned her head quickly toward him. "What are you doing here? How did you find me?"

"Brian gave me the name of the town and your husband's last name; I took it from there. I couldn't let you leave without telling you how much you mean to me. I did not think anyone had the ability to understand the pain I felt after losing Elizabeth until you told me about yours. I'm ashamed of myself at how selfish I acted. I allowed myself to indulge in self-pity. You gave me the strength and incentive to make peace with my loss. Let me do the same for you. I cannot imagine another day without you in my life. I am here to take you home where you belong."

She started to cry. "I don't belong anywhere."

He placed his hands on her knees and knelt before her. "You belong with me. I love you and I know you love me too."

She made no attempt to wipe away the tears dripping from her eyes that fell onto her shirt. "I don't deserve to love anyone. I not only didn't save Philip, but I'm also the one who killed him."

A voice from behind them said, "An unholy war with cowardly enemies killed Philip, not you." It was Nora's mother-in-law speaking. "I don't know where you got the idea you aren't entitled to love again when it's all you've ever given." She bent over Nora taking her hand. "You have been given another chance, take it. There is no disloyalty to Philip and certainly you cannot believe we don't want you to be happy."

Nora once told Ben he was not being disloyal to his daughter if he let himself be happy. Those words seemed hollow when she was faced with the same dilemma. "But what about you and Don?"

"What about us? I don't expect you to forget you have parents who love you, and we're only a day's drive away. If Philip had lived, our daily lives would have been the same. We would visit, spend holidays together, and talk on a regular basis." She looked at Ben and said, "I assume we're welcome in your home."

He never hugged anyone tighter than he did Pat.

"I'll drive you there myself."

"I don't know if I can ever be the person you need or want," Nora said in a broken voice.

"You are that person; you don't have to change a thing. Honestly, I did not know how much longer I'd have hidden behind Elizabeth's death to keep from living again. I shut everyone out." Then he smiled and added, "Except Brian, no one can shut him out."

Despite her emotional pain and the seriousness of their conversation, she smiled at the reference to Brian and nodded in response.

Ben continued, "Brian never gave up on me. I was sometimes brutal with him because I wanted to be left alone in my darkness. I drowned myself in my work, which made me prosper, but also insulated me with the perpetual excuses of, 'I've got a deadline.' Eventually everyone left me alone, just like my ex-wife—everyone except Brian. He was my candle in a dark room, but you threw open the windows, figuratively and literally. You gave me hope, and I am no longer that sad, unapproachable person I was when we met. It scares me how much similarity there was between the way we dealt with our grief."

Nora sniffled and dabbed at her eyes with her sleeve. "It's not the same thing."

Shaking his head and staring at her with penetrating eyes, his voice became stern in tone. "It is exactly the same thing. What happened to you and me were circumstances completely out of our control, but we took responsibility for them anyway. So many times, I chastised myself by saying, 'I should have taken Lizzie to the doctor sooner. I should have known her cold and fever was something serious. I cost her precious time when she might have been treated.' These were all things I've played out in my head over and over for years. I was incapable of understanding terrible things happen to good people."

"Elizabeth was an innocent child, and you had no part in her death," Nora reminded him.

"I am not even going to try to minimize what you went through, except to remind you the result was the same. We were two people left behind to deal with our survivor's guilt. I will always carry Lizzie in my heart. It is the first time I understood when my ex-wife said she only wanted to remember the joy. What's the point of her life, if not to celebrate it. You must feel the same way about Philip. Don't dwell on how he died, remember how he lived."

"What if I can't? What if I am too damaged?" she whispered in a tone of desperation.

"I don't believe that. Let me ask you something; despite why you came to work for me, were you happy this past year?"

She was silent for a moment, then replied, "I was."

"Why?" he asked rhetorically.

She took a deep breath. "I could be me with without judgement or pity."

Taking her hand, he placed it to his lips and kissed it. "That's my point; I fell in love with the real Nora, not the one you have been trying to run from. Come home with me. Now there are no secrets between us, we can start our lives over. We have so much to offer each other."

"Do you think it's that simple?"

"Yes, I do; it's that simple. Many times, the problems are complex, but the solutions are not. You have said you thought you were a coward. You have been anything but cowardly. It took the same courage to stand by Philip as it did for him to fight in the war. Use that courage to fight for yourself, for us."

"What if I let you down?"

He shrugged. "I am not worried about that, because we have gone through so much already. Half the battle is knowing where you want to be, not where you've been. I want to be with you. We can still honor Lizzie and Philip by continuing our support for causes which lend support to their respective situations. We can still have a life together. I have already seen we are stronger together than apart."

****

She was forced to admit to herself it was true. When Vincent died, Ben was a comfort at her side throughout the funeral. He was there because he knew it was important for her to honor him. She did the same thing for him at the banquet when he broke down after receiving the award.

"I'm tired of feeling like there is a heavy weight on my shoulders. I'm tired of reliving bad memories, and I'm tired of being tired," she cried.

He smiled. "Then come home with me and you won't be tired any longer."

This time when Nora watched her hometown as it disappeared in her rearview mirror, she was not running away from it, she was running toward something better.

A word about the author...

Writing is a second act for C. Ellen Culverwell; her first was law enforcement. After earning a degree in criminal justice, she was hired as the youngest and among the first women to be a Niagara County deputy sheriff. After leaving the force to raise her daughter, she continued to consult with various law enforcement agencies in matters of electronic surveillance. After the death of her husband, she turned to her passion for writing. Originally, her writing was meant to be cathartic, a means to empower her imagination. Her mantra has become, "Personal tragedy is only tragic when it's not chapter one."

She lives with her daughter on their horse farm in their ancestral hometown of Newfane, New York, minutes from majestic Niagara Falls. Mother and daughter are currently experimenting with scent training their horses for search, rescue, and recovery. Her cast of characters reflects both people she has met while in law enforcement and members of her close-knit community. They are and will continue to be her inspiration to create new storylines and interesting characters.

You may reach C. Ellen Culverwell at:
www.cellenculverwell.com

Thank you for purchasing
this publication of The Wild Rose Press, Inc.

For questions or more information
contact us at
info@thewildrosepress.com.

The Wild Rose Press, Inc.
www.thewildrosepress.com